~~

ALOHA

~~

Tiwaka

~ goes to ~

Waikiki

The Life and Times of a Hawaiian Tiki Bar

book 3

Everett Peacock

visit

theParrotTalksInChocolate.com

and

listen to the **Radio Tiwaka !**

Tiki and Alternative Rock just like they play in the bar!

ISBN 1468026976 / EAN-13 978-1468026979

cover art by: Kerne Erickson

KEricksonArt.com

proofreading: Valentina Cano

v.2

Other books by the Author

~~

The Life and Times of a Hawaiian Tiki Bar

book 1: The Parrot Talks In Chocolate

book 2: In the Middle of the Third Planet's
          Most Wonderful of Oceans

book 3: Tiwaka Goes to Waikiki

book 4: Green Bananas

~~

Death by Facebook

~~

Escaping the Magnificent

~~

Escape from Hanalei

~~

The Galactics

~~

A Paradise of One

~ ~ ~

for all those in love

with something larger

than themselves

~ ~ ~

PREFACE

When I wrote the first book in this series, The Parrot Talks in Chocolate, I was having a little fun while waiting on my first novel to exit editing (it has yet to do so!). While I was anxiously awaiting for my scifi medical thriller to begin making sense to its first readers, I would climb up into my tree house in the jungles of Haiku, Maui, Hawaii. Every morning, quite a bit before sunrise, big Kona coffee filled Lee Ceramic mug in hand I made my way thirty feet up into the top of our banyan. My house Wi-Fi signal breached the distance tickling my laptop just enough to give me access to my cloud based music.

The vast expanse of open ocean spread out before the sun, from Hana in the southeast across my view to Molokai in the northwest. The clear summit of Haleakala stood guard over it all behind me, all while my beautiful wife and kids slept soundly in our tiny cabin with our dogs, cats and crickets (we kept them caged in the bathroom for their songs and to keep the geckos from eating them).

The fantasy flowed easily up there in the early light, as if I had already lived the story. Of course I had not. Not all of it. When I sell my millionth copy in this series I *will* build the bar, adopt a parrot and install the solar panels to power the tree house restaurant and the electric pickup truck. All the other details in the stories have a good deal of truth to them.

Watch for the invitation, soon, to Tiwaka's Tiki Bar & Grill.

Just be sure to tip the parrot.

Everett Peacock
November 30, 2011
Kula, Maui, Hawaii

~~

Dedicated to

my wife Della

for proving to me, time and time again,

that positive thoughts produce positive results,

for inspiring my universe with three wonderful children

who continuously remind me of a greater cause,

who cooks the best pasta this side of the Moon,

and

for paying all the bills

while I was hanging out at Tiwaka's

for three years now

~~

CONTENTS

~~

~~~

Christmas Miracles

Tiwaka had for the past two or three months been getting up quite early, wobbling outside before anyone else and as the sun would rise, spread and flex his wings, repeatedly. I only discovered this by accident when I had come back early from a pre-dawn no-surf surf outing. My favorite bird, the bar's namesake and my dearest friend was up to something.

Now it was Christmas morning, again without any waves, and I had put my board back into the naupaka hedge intending to go back to bed when I spied his colorful little body at the top of the trail leading to Ococ's cliff side grave. He looked back at me as he flapped his magnificence. I waved back and turned to give him his privacy.

It was sad in a way. His wing muscles had been damaged when he had been severely clipped as a baby back in Honolulu, preventing his ever being able to fly.

That curse would be akin to me not being able to surf, despite living next to the beach and watching all my friends slide down the perfect waves of our secret break, Unknowns. Poor Tiwaka was surrounded by thousands of flying birds in the jungle, flying insects and on occasion flying humans skirting the treetops on ultralights. I always wondered how he must handle that.

Tiwaka though had one significant advantage over just about every other living creature I had ever encountered. He was a dreamer, a dreamer with a plan. If he thought sunrise wing stretches would bring back his power to fly, then hallelujah to that! He was over twenty-five years old, middle age for his lot, at this point but there was nothing, in my mind, that said life restricted its magic to the young.

I climbed the stairs up to my still warm bed at the top of the tree house and snuggled in next to Sandy. In moments I was dreaming about as vividly as I could ever remember ...

I was waxing up my eight foot mini-tanker board on the sand of some distant beach. Tiwaka was standing about mid board staring out toward the lineup of waves. There was music, something psychedelic, maybe Pictures of Matchstick Men, by Status Quo, which has some great 60's guitar riffs. In one of those quirks of dreams I even had the music I wanted to hear marked, 1:16 to 1:54.

At 1:26 Tiwaka took two stomps forward on his feet, left and right, paused and took two more, up to the nose of the board where he spread an incredible wingspan. It was much larger than anything I had ever seen him sport before, wings of a flyer!

Fade right into the next scene where a cinematographer might be, watching me drop in on a late drop on an overhead wave. Glassy water held the edge of my board as I made a tight bottom turn and lined up for what was going to be a great barrel. Right before the lip launched out over my head, at 1:43 actually, Tiwaka swooped in from off camera, over my head, banked just before the wall of the wave, spread his wings and braked perfectly, landing right on the nose of my board.

Tucking his wings in tight and crouching low for the ride, the cinematographer got a great shot of one of his talons flexing into a shaka sign as we both slid past, in slow motion of course!

... Sandy woke me gently from this with one of her signature kisses, something so sweet and exotic I felt like I was going from one dream to another.

"Merry Christmas darling," she whispered.

I blinked a couple of times, until I felt my grin moving up to my eyes. "Ho Ho Ho honey!" Sitting up I looked over to where six month old baby Kiawe was pointing out the window cooing and jumping up and down.

"Bird. Birdy!" she said.

Both Sandy and I jumped up, completely blown away by Kiawe's very first words! What a Christmas present this was! Tiwaka would love that those words were 'bird'.

"Bird?" Sandy said, recovering from her shock first.

"Birdy, birdy!" Kiawe said again and again, pointing out the window.

Sandy looked to where the pink sky was kissing the tops of the jungle below and gasped.

"What is it honey?" I was holding Kiawe now, patting her incredibly smooth skin, walking over to the window where Sandy was now also pointing.

There I saw bright colors climbing into the cool clear air, turning into wider and wider circles. Something was painting the sky with vibrant reds, yellows and blue. It couldn't be! I couldn't find the words, couldn't bring my mind to acknowledge the miracle, but Sandy finally did.

"It's Tiwaka!"

Kona Storm

Some five hundred forty some odd miles away, along a map line connecting Maui to Tahiti there was something else circling. It wasn't nearly as colorful as a middle aged parrot but they both did have a lot in common.

Tiwaka was humming some avian favorite as he stretched his arms farther and farther into the tropical air. So was this other creation of nature, vibrating the very sky with increasingly large updrafts of air. It was the same song of celebration, chant like breaths of self awareness, a fresh realization of new life.

Every new flier, jubilation coursing through their veins, strives for more altitude. The air is sweeter and the stars closer. Confidence pushes higher and higher, carried on the new found power to push farther, to go where no one else might find you.

Both the parrot and the massive pool of warm rising air aimed for the same deep blues of tropical sky, back lit by the dark kiss of space.

~~~

Hōkūle'a-2, spinning itself two degrees east-southeast to maximize its view, was also aiming for those same deep blue tropical skies. Sensors and cameras focused on rapidly increasing flashes of lightning filling thickening anvils of cumulus. The large population of Honolulu, and the military installations of Pearl Harbor and Hickam Air Force Base, were all keenly aware of how desperate escape might be from a small island. Preparation was their only hope.

Weather Specialist First Class Kenji Saito, fresh from orbital mechanics school, sat back after successfully aiming his 2200 pound weather satellite exactly where it was needed. The fact that he got it perfect on the first try might have been a bigger deal last year. However with the new Peacock 3K-B Solar Ion thrusters on board, generating a 3kW ion stream from what it collected from its solar panels alone, fuel was never going to be a consideration again. In fact the new Hōkūle'a series of satellites were quickly becoming training platforms for every new space cadet from Washington to Beijing. Mistakes in navigation no longer consumed precious finite fuel supplies.

Kenji sat back in his chair and took the few moments of quiet to take a deep breath. A neglected plate lunch of shoyu ahi poke and maki sushi remained well chilled in the air conditioning. It would have to wait until he could fashion up a report for CINCPAC fleet at Pearl Harbor and their newest subscriber.

The cameras on the relatively low flying bird focused on their slowly moving target. Geosynchronous orbits, 22,000 miles above the sea surface were no longer used to save fuel at the expense of resolution. Now, the new birds, the Hōkūle'as, flew much lower, dodging the phone satellites and the Virgin Galactic tourists. They were low enough to where cameras and radar could practically feel their way around.

There wasn't enough time to take a second relaxing deep breath before the live images began marching across his monitors. Kenji punched in a few standard requests based on what he saw initially. REQUEST: rotational analysis. REQUEST: cloud top ping. REQUEST: thermal signature. REQUEST: lightning count.

He had seen this before, at least a hundred times. The great liquid oceans were bleeding off their excess heat directly into the adjoining oceans of air. It was an incredible dance of energy. The sun dropped untold quantities of energy into the seas daily and in the amazing balance of nature it would be funneled back up. The great hurricanes, once up and spinning could release through condensation a massive 6.0×10^{14} watts of energy. Daily. A meaningless number until you considered it is 200 times the world's electrical generating capacity. Daily.

Kenji peered down at his results, now filtering up from the servers two floors below his comfortable high back captain's chair.

ROTATIONAL ANALYSIS COMPLETE: 5 degrees per hour.

CLOUD TOP PING COMPLETE: 57,565 feet

THERMAL SIGNATURE COMPLETE: Stage 3 Maturity +

LIGHTNING COUNT COMPLETE: 65 per min/square mile

The widening weather system didn't seem to be moving in any particular direction, and that was a problem. It had been born atop a pool of warm ocean and there it sat soaking up even more energy. With the rotation of the earth kicking in a counter clockwise swirl would soon develop beyond the 5 degrees recorded so far.

Weather Specialist First Class Kenji Saito crafted an analysis message to both CINCPAC fleet in Pearl Harbor and Virgin Galactic Dispatch in Las Cruces. "Hawaiian islands subject to tropical weather within next 36 hours. Advise against using harbors and airports as alternates. Virgin flights approaching from the south advised to immediately abdicate to Papeete or Anchorage."

That done, he turned to his neglected shoyu ahi poke and maki sushi . The supplied chop sticks worked delicately pinching some of each. As he enjoyed the seasoned raw fish and rice he noticed more activity on his monitors. Vertical lightning sprites from the top most cumulus giants were reaching straight out into space for his satellite.

"Wow," Kenji whispered. "You're a feisty one."

~ ~ ~

Empty Nest

Sandy couldn't help her smile; it was so wide she could barely talk to Tiwaka, fresh from his first flight.

"You're a feisty one!"

Baby Kiawe wiggled at the words, thinking of course they were meant for her. Sandy switched the baby to her other hip and reached down to stroke the iridescent feathers.

"When did you learn to fly Tiwaka?" Sandy sat on the bamboo bench next to the near exhausted parrot. "We thought you had been permanently clipped back when you were a baby," the last words giving her a shiver and forcing a protective hug and kiss to Kiawe's silky hair.

Tiwaka looked up to the Tahitian beauty and blinked once, then glanced to her hip, with its mushroom of beauty squirming there. He tapped his feet a couple of times, trying to work the word up from deep inside. Shaking his legs and moving his wings back slightly, despite their incredible weakness now, he threw his head back a little and looked to his left, toward the sea cliffs.

That's where I found my little family early Christmas afternoon as I walked up the guava paved dirt path leading back from Unknowns, and a rising swell of small waves. The three most wonderful things in my universe, a universe crowded with wonderful infinities, sat together on the lower deck of our tree house home.

"Your turn baby!" I announced. With a young baby, it was difficult to get a surf session together lately. Someone had to always entertain baby Kiawe.

"No worries, I'll go later. Maybe when Ma and Pa can watch her, we can go together?"

I leaned over the railing and kissed my two girls, leaving a little salt water from the sea on each of their foreheads. My hair must have still held a pint of the Pacific Ocean.

"Perfect," I thought, amazed at Sandy's capacity to come up with the best solution. Feeling a little guilty now for having surfed alone I slid my board into the naupaka hedge, shook my head a bit and sat down on the other side of Tiwaka.

"Have you asked him about his flying?"

"Birdy!" Kiawe squealed again, pointing at the foot stomping collection of colors.

"Looks like he is trying ..." I added.

"I asked him when he learned to fly..." Sandy answered at the same moment.

We both paused as Tiwaka worked hard to find his words, shivering and shaking and stomping. If we didn't know him better we would have feared he was having a seizure. In a lot of ways it was similar. Tiwaka's brain signals didn't really have a path to vocalization like we did, especially when he was responding to unscripted questions.

A thousand macaws like him had memorized a thousand words, but none, as far as I knew, could use language like Tiwaka. He "understood" language and didn't just react to cues with memorized responses. Of course, it came with a price. Evolution had not quite finished its work with him, and the words he knew he wanted to use had to be pulled, kicking and fighting, through the primitive areas of his avian brain until they could be processed in his speech center.

An analogy I liked to tell at the bar when people asked about Tiwaka's challenge with words went like this: A human talking was like me walking back along my nice well worn path to the beach. The path was well marked and easy to use. With Tiwaka it was more akin to pushing through the thickest jungle off to the side of that path, vines and mud and juicy bugs all distracting him along the way. If it wasn't for his herculean tenacity Tiwaka would be just another handsome bar bird.

Tiwaka was still stomping his feet, like he was trying to get some unseen jungle mud off his talons. Suddenly, as if he needed to bleed off some energy he opened his wings fully, the tips fluttering like a drummer's sticks. His head leaned back as he stared at the sky above and he took one step forward, followed by his other foot. He took another two step, looked over to Sandy and exclaimed.

"Two!"

She looked at me raising her shoulders and I shook my head slowly. The poor bird was no doubt tired from flying and here he was expending a huge amount of his remaining energy just to talk to us. Whatabird!

I looked at my long time friend with a big heaping bucket full of compassion. He was trying so hard, pushing the limits of what his DNA said he was capable of doing. If anything he was the hardest working bird on the planet, and I could say with some authority that he beat a few people I knew.

Tiwaka often broke his words into pieces. It was easier to get them out that way I guess. Talking with him was a lot like playing Scrabble. So, I quickly went into game mode.

"Tuesday?" I volunteered. Not likely, it was Sunday now and we would have noticed him flying before now if he had started five days ago. "Two...morrow?" No, that didn't work either.

"Too," Sandy said, "like too much? Maybe my question was too much?"

We both shook our heads no, he had answered more difficult questions. I quickly thought a piece of milk chocolate protecting a large Brazil nut might work and turned to look toward the bar.

Tiwaka was shaking, stomping and shivering. Baby Kiawe hugged Sandy a little tighter and I thought about taking a step back. I might have but I thought I might need to catch the poor bird if he fell off the bench. Just then his wings couldn't hold out any longer. Wrapping them around his chest, in a hug, he got out another word.

"Day!"

"Day?" I repeated, like a parrot might.

Baby Kiawe was now squirming and waving her arm, no doubt enjoying the show. Sandy switched her to her other hip, a beautiful movement of color and feminine grace a father would never grow tired of. But, my distraction was short lived.

"Two days?" Sandy asked me. "Maybe he's been flying for two days?"

I shook my head slowly. Maybe so.

Baby Kiawe was now bouncing off of Sandy's hip, pushing herself up and down and waving her one free arm like a wing. Tiwaka folded his own wings back and turned to look at the baby, nodding his head back and forth slowly.

Cooing and drooling and the occasional burp from our little package of wonder was common, but lately Baby Kiawe had been vocalizing dozens of cute sounds, all variations of something ending in the "e" sound. Hers was the sing song language we all adopt in the beginning.

Tiwaka took a step toward Baby Kiawe, bobbing his head a little more now. I saw Sandy unconsciously move a tiny bit backward along the bamboo seat, careful to keep our featherless baby away from our feathered one.

Baby Kiawe was cooing loudly now, looking right at Tiwaka, then up to me, swinging around to look at Sandy, slinging drool and laughing. Her arm was practically wind milling around, forcing Sandy to dodge a couple of errant rotations.

Tiwaka, still looking at Baby Kiawe, raised one foot slowly and stomped it down on the bamboo. Baby Kiawe did the same, pushing her little toes into Sandy's thigh, laughing even louder now. Before Sandy or I could comment on the amazing show, our little baby, our little creation, our permanent bridge to all that is crazy wonderful about being alive spoke clearly and distinctly.

"To-day." Her arm waving stopped and she looked up from the parrot to me. "Today," she repeated. Baby Kiawe turned to look at her mama, who was tearing up with joy and hugging her, smearing drool all over her shoulder.

Tiwaka turned back to look at me and nodded his head up once, like anyone at the bar might when silently sharing something. I looked at my long time friend Tiwaka, my wonderful wife and our incredible baby. I was relishing this moment, of course. Yet, there was a layer to it I had never felt before. It was a painful twinge tugging at my heart, telling me that this was something I would always remember, even as an old man. But, there was a dark side - it would never be repeated.

A shiver moved through me, like a spirit might stirring the air around me. I suddenly was able to see the future, a future where it wasn't just me anymore, where it wasn't just Sandy and I laughing in the hammock, or Tiwaka and I serving up dozens of Coco Loco Moco on a rocking Saturday night. It was a future that was awesome, but different. It was decidedly a future where first words were only spoken once.

I leaned over and hugged Baby Kiawe tightly as she squirmed on Sandy's leg. I could feel something different now in our embrace, and it wasn't just the drool. It was a new perspective I had never noticed in myself. I was somehow different now. A baby can do that to you. You see, babies are masters of change.

These incredible moments with Baby Kiawe were sweeter than anything I could have ever imagined, but they were fleeting. There would be more cool moments no doubt, but there would only be one moment where it was a first for her. Her first words, her first steps - my first revelation that some things don't repeat, like the surf or the rain does.

Perhaps it was my newfound concept of time, now that I had a family and could see how nature provides for a continuum. One day Tiwaka would pass on, like Ococ had. One day Baby Kiawe would hate that name, and then eventually one day leave our tree house. It was all part of a long line of wonderful things that moved in a single direction.

I had never really been aware of a direction to time before. It had always been a circular concept. The sun came up, we surfed, it got hot we took a nap, the sun set and the bar opened. The sun came back up the next day and we did it all again. Winter brought big surf, summer brought good diving and then it repeated, again and again. Paradise had always been circular, consistent.

Baby Kiawe had spoken her first words this week. But, there would never be a week again where she would speak her first words. That was over. Yes, there would be other cool "firsts" but that linear quality to time was manifesting itself now in ways I had never really understood. It was making the magic bittersweet.

I felt myself falling into a pit of despair despite knowing I should embrace these moments. As if on cue, my friend, my confident, my mentor of all things relevant pulled me out and away from the abyss, once again. Tiwaka turned to me, looking at me first with his left eye and then with his right and said the one word that would define the rest of my existence, if I could manage to let it do so.

"Today!"

~~~

Today

"Can you believe that honey?" Sandy asked. "Tiwaka only learned to fly today?" She hoisted Baby Kiawe over to her other hip.

"Here," I reached for our baby, being sure to grasp her securely under her armpits. She was drooling all over her smooth and now slippery baby skin. "Let me hold this little critter." I saw a towel draped over the bamboo frame of our bed and went to get it.

"Honestly, Tiwaka," Sandy said taking the towel from me and wiping her skin dry. "I am so proud of you!"

Tiwaka threw his chest out, as he was fond of doing when feeling big and important. His wings soon followed and as he threw his head back I went to cover Baby Kiawe's ears.

"Squaaaaaawk!"

I know it's probably impossible to see a smile on a beak, but I swear I saw one on Tiwaka. His eyes were twinkling as he ate up the praise and admiration.

"You da bird!" I exclaimed in my best fatherly tone. I held out my hand for a high five. He hit me back with a dozen feathers.

"Today?" I asked Tiwaka. I was hugging and kissing Baby Kiawe's soft hair as I looked at the parrot.

He nodded and folded his wings back, turning his head to watch me with each eye. It was as if each eye showed him something different from the other. This habit of his always made me think he was looking more intimately at me. I wondered if one eye showed him my *true intentions* and the other eye showed him my *dreams*. I laughed silently to myself at that thought. Sure. It was more likely one eye was better than the other and he was only confirming what the other was seeing.

Baby Kiawe had a handful of my curls and I had to peel them out of her grasp, but when I looked back at Tiwaka he was watching me now with only one eye. It must be the one that looked into my dreams.

"Let's go out to the hammock," I offered. We had a few hours before the bar opened for Christmas dinner. "All of us," I held out my hand to Tiwaka.

Quickly, he looked at my hand with his other eye, the *true intentions* one, and figured it was safe.

A few minutes later I was following Sandy and her small backpack full of baby necessities down the groovy grass trail to the sea cliffs. Baby Kiawe was on my left hip and Tiwaka was perched on my right forearm. I had a good flex going on to hold both of them. Thankfully, we made it to the hammock before I had to admit I needed a rest stop.

Sandy slid the backpack off her bronzed shoulders as if she had been dancing with it, letting it gracefully land softly in the grass. Her back was still to me as she glanced toward the sea.

The mother thing had only enhanced her appearance, but then I *was* partial. She had shed what little extra weight she had put on and was back to pre-pregnancy form, save for one interesting change. Sandy's tube tops had all needed replacing.

"Here," she asked, holding her hands out for Baby Kiawe. "She must be hungry by now."

I gave my right arm a little twist and Tiwaka got the hint to glide down to the ground. Handing Baby Kiawe off to Sandy I watched her roll down her tube top to her waist.

"How do you know?" I asked without trying to stare more than fascination would dictate.

Sandy looked up at me, grinning. Baby Kiawe was already latched on to her left breast.

"It's easy, darling." Sandy leaned back in the hammock getting comfortable. I sat down on the soft grass next to them, Tiwaka moved over closer as well.

"When I'm full..." she looked down to her chest, then back up to me. "...she's hungry." Sandy laughed. "Works out just right, don't you think?"

I shook my head and smiled. "Ain't nature grand!"

Tiwaka whistled like I had taught him when the Canadian nurses used to dance topless at the bar.

"Tiwaka!" I whispered. "Not the time and place dude!"

I looked over to Sandy, who knew that whistle well, and we both laughed so hard Baby Kiawe fell right off her meal train. That got me laughing even harder and I fell back into the grass.

Tiwaka immediately jumped up on my chest and announced in his best Elvis voice, "I love you boss! Bigtime!"

Baby Kiawe took note of the action and pulled away long enough to laugh and say "Birdie!" before getting back to business.

Finally, I rolled back up to a sitting position, pushing the feathers off to the side, gently. Sandy smiled at me for just a moment before looking back to her hungry baby. Tiwaka sat at my feet and bobbed his head in some silent rhythm only he could hear.

I could hear a rhythm as well, visualized it as it were. The trade winds were moving nicely up the cliff face and over to our place between the guava trees, moving the hammock lightly and filling my lungs with the lightest taste of ocean. That perfect balance of warm sunshine and light shade reminded me of all that my world used to be: repeating patterns of beauty.

Yet, there was Baby Kiawe, growing and changing daily. I might find the shade of the guava trees in my hammock another thousand times, but I wouldn't find Baby Kiawe nursing from my beautiful wife another month. For a moment, that fear invaded my peace again. A fear that these magical moments would soon escape me. This new bad habit time had suddenly demonstrated, its linear feature would keep me from coming back to these moments again and again.

I lay back into the grass, hoping to hide my distress from Sandy and the baby. Tiwaka though was having none of it and hopped right back up on my chest, took two steps forward and bent his head down to look me directly in the eye. First his left and then his right eye gazed into mine.

"Tiwaka, give me a moment will you?" I whispered.

Just behind his feathered concern, in the sky directly above, I saw the rapid movement of clouds streaking the blue with their silent white songs. The sun sparkled a moment as it peeked out from behind guava leaves, touching my face with just a kiss of warmth before retreating. The groovy grass cushioned my head, nestled in my hands, with a soft pillow that never itched, never cut.

Baby Kiawe was cooing softly next to me and Sandy began singing a quiet Tahitian song, rocking next to me. Tiwaka was still staring at me, stomping his feet lightly against my chest, letting me know he was still waiting for my attention.

It was so special, so beautiful, so transient I couldn't hold back a little tear, despite Tiwaka's uncomfortable inspection of my face. How was I ever going to resolve this problem? This sadness in the very heart of joy?

The answer was close. About three inches away from my nose and switching eyes constantly.

"Boss," Tiwaka said, or asked. I never could be quite sure.

"Yes, Tiwaka?" I whispered, trying to keep my issues as private as I could.

The parrot reached down to grasp my shirt collar with his beak and pulled me up, to a sitting position. Once I was up, he hopped down to the groovy grass and spread his magnificent wings as far as he could.

Sandy took notice and looked over to me, smiling.

My brother from another mother turned around in a complete circle, looked to me and said in his best American accent, "Today."

He then flew up to the hammock spreader bar and said it again, "Today."

After that he flew up to the lowest guava limb, looked down at all three of us and said it yet again, "Today."

"He sure seems proud of his learning to fly today, doesn't he?" Sandy laughed.

I nodded, but I was getting a different message. I wasn't quite sure until he walked to the edge of the cliff, some twenty feet away. I thought he might launch off into flight, but he held steady on the edge, letting the up rushing trade winds rustle his feathers. Looking back to me, first with the eye on *my true intentions* and then the eye toward *my dreams* he squawked loudly, clearly and without a doubt, "Today!"

That was it! The parrot had it right, again.

"Silly bird!" Sandy laughed again, but my kiss stopped her short. My hands went to Baby Kiawe's soft silky hair, caressing her like the miracle she truly was.

Sandy laughed again, kissed me again and said softly, "Isn't today the most wonderful day?"

"Yes, it couldn't get any more perfect."

The parrot had made his point. Today, each day, would be my new definition of time. There would be no future, only today, only now. That solved that silly linear issue and let me live like I was used to, in the moment.

A few tears invaded my eyes and Sandy, ever loving and wise simply kissed them away and whispered into my ear, "I love you."

Baby Kiawe burped her concurrence.

~~~

The Parrot Who Rode the Thunder

In Honolulu, Weather Specialist First Class Kenji Saito was about to sign off his weather station computer. His relief had shown up early and when her coffee was ready she would send him on his way, another twelve hour shift done.

His report was done, his alerts had been sent and knowing what he knew he would go back to his apartment and bring his lanai plants inside. He might go next door and let old Mrs. Canterbury know it might be a good idea to bring her lawn chair in. Other than that, he would just let KGMB TV tell everyone else when their daily five o'clock 'Severe Weather' feature got to finally talk about some severe weather.

"So Kenji," Weather Specialist Second Class Amber Smith asked. "What's with this burp southwest of Maui?"

He laughed at little at that. Burp was a good analogy, all right. The ocean was burping out quite a bit of energy into the gaseous sea that rested just on top of its surface.

"We've got a touch of rotation, fifty-five thousand for tops and no shear in sight." Kenji stood up and gave her the chair. "You're gonna be busy tonight Amber. Looks like my weekend hikes are gonna get canceled."

Amber scanned the monitors, Kenji's report synopsis and chugged the rest of her coffee.

"Too bad" she said under her breath. "You're gonna be on trail repair duty for a month after this one Kenji."

~~~

The dawn arrived without the usual fanfare of orange, yellows and bird calls. In fact, it was a bit late showing up. Thick gray layers of fast moving clouds practically hugged the ocean surface, rushing toward the sea cliffs, the tree house, the bar and a little used path into the jungle.

Tiwaka didn't need much light to find his way, but it was still difficult walking uphill picking as dry a route as possible through the new mud. Overhanging passion fruit vines made flight through this part of the jungle near impossible.

It was darker here, jungle dark, with spits of rain finding their way all the way through to his feathers. Wind moving spastically through the higher branches overhead had all but the most terrified little birds keeping quiet.

The magnificently colored parrot could hear little peeps and squeaks from the young birds shivering in the tree branches above. He stopped and glanced up. A deep, resonating squawk comforted them, feeling good coming from deep inside his belly. Tiwaka felt himself a mature creature lately, generous with his advice for the young ones. It also imbued him with a strong duty to pay his respects to a dead friend.

Finally reaching the east facing cliff, a grand opening in the jungle, he found the small bamboo cross draped with kukui nut lei. "Ococ" was fading a bit from the year of weathering.

Half leaping and half flying he made it to the top of the cross, firmly grasping the bamboo. The deep valley below was full of ghostly mist rising from warm depths meeting the cold air from the approaching storm. Waterfalls were already sweeping over the green walls, falling silver and clear celebrations of water and gravity. Thunder, deep and rolling, could be heard moving off to the far southwest.

Tiwaka bent over to grasp the first of the two kukui nut lei and moved it to the left side of the cross. He did the same with the remaining lei, moving it to the right side. Comfortable in his ritual he opened his wings fully, balancing himself against the occasional breath of wind.

There, on top of the old bamboo cross, in weather similar to that which had accompanied the old dog from this world to the next, Tiwaka opened his soul to search for his friend Ococ ... and found him.

The parrot's heart went out to his friend, somewhere in that place where they had been able to find each other. I'm sure Tiwaka's scalp tingled like mine would have at the experience.

Another little gust of wind moved through the jungle, this one a bit stronger than the last. Tiwaka kept his balance, grasping the bamboo a little tighter.

"I can fly," Tiwaka said out loud. "Ococ..." he paused in yet another burst of wind. "...I can fly!"

Somewhere, deep inside a part of Tiwaka that I never knew existed anywhere but in people, he heard a friendly growl, an encouragement. Anyone else might have heard a loud clap of impossibly deep thunder echoing from high up on Haleakala, rolling down through the valley.

Anyone else, myself included, might have thought the next burst of wind just an acceleration of the storm. Tiwaka though felt it as a gentle nudge, and as he leapt off the cross and out over the cliff's edge, he heard his friend say "Fly!"

~~~

Baby Kiawe had perfect timing. Every sunrise a new diaper would be summoned. I was up fulfilling that request as well as taking an extra moment to check the weather.

Normally, these kind of mornings were too delicious to get out of bed for, and after dressing baby girl, I would normally leap back under the covers with Sandy. I would have but the wind was calling.

I climbed up to the top of the tree house to check Unknowns, if not for surf at least for some measure of what the ocean was doing. My first clue of a storm was the light rain swirling all around my perch. The deck up there was soaked. The leaves on the banyan tree just outside were fluttering briskly, launching themselves on one way trips to the jungle floor below.

The bay at Unknowns was what the old timers used to call "Victory at Sea". I had finally asked someone about that name and they told me to Google it. Apparently, during the '50s there had been a documentary film made in the US about our warships plowing through the Pacific Ocean on their way to kick some WWII butt. The ocean was raucous and threatening then, just as it looked now. Massive waves were slamming into the cliffs on either side of the bay, casting great sheets of spray high into the air, adding more gray to what the sky had already provided.

I turned to look toward the south, where the weather seemed to be coming from. It was a nasty looking dark sky, somewhere between left over nighttime and upcoming rain. My eyes saw something a bit unusual. I looked a little harder thinking I was seeing a frothing movement in the clouds, a cold boiling in the sky.

As I marveled at the spectacle my eyes caught movement rocketing up from the valley near Ococ's grave. It was still a bit dark to make it out, but it was something solid moving steeply upward. Just above it the clouds were swirling in a strange way, looking a lot like the beginnings of a small waterspout.

I watched, fascinated, as other small stuff, maybe leaves and such, followed the first object up toward the base of the swirling mass of clouds. Behind me, to the east, the sun took a brief second to peer through the clouds.

"Rainbow!" I instinctively said to myself. The mists in the valley caught it just right splashing an arch with the red, orange, yellow, green, blue, indigo and violet.

Below me I heard Baby Kiawe stirring, cooing in a sweet little baby dream no doubt. As I turned back to check out the valley, I saw that first object approach the bottom of the cloud and flutter there for a moment. As it did so, I caught a different but quite familiar splash of color.

My heart practically stopped, right before it began racing.

"That's no rainbow!"

~~~

Fear seems to come in two flavors. The most common is the one based in knowledge – we know the third rail of a subway train track will electrocute us. So, we fear touching it. The other flavor though is quite a bit more powerful, being based on innate survival instincts. Falling from a great height is programmed very well into our minds. We fear falling even as babies.

Consider how much more powerful instinct is. Which makes you sweat more, thinking about that third rail, or standing in the open door of a small airplane at 12,000 feet? Innate fears, even when confronted with knowledge can still terrify you. Take skydiving. Knowledge tells you the parachute will certainly save you but that instinct rooted in your DNA that says falling is dangerous still grips your heart with both hands.

I imagine birds feel the falling instinct more intensely than non-fliers. You see when a bird flies he has both fears to process. There is the knowledge based flavor that tells them they must at all times be flapping those wings or gliding on them. And, there is the survival instinct that tells them that they are at great heights where a fall will mean certain destruction.

It's a lot like people and driving cars. We process both fears through our justification process. Knowledge tells us that moving at sixty miles per hour in a metal/plastic contraption full of volatile fuel is fine, as long as nothing unexpected happens. Open the door and look out at the ground sweeping by and your instincts send you a strong message ... don't step out.

I suppose whenever we are in motion, bird or bartender, there is danger.

Tiwaka, despite being new to the flying thing understood both flavors of fear quite well. And maybe there was a third flavor manifesting inside his increasingly terrified avian brain.

He shouldn't have skipped breakfast!

~~~

Storm prep at the bar was always a losing battle against geography. Kona storms were pretty rare, we might go a year or two without even getting one. Yet, as most islanders knew, the biggest problem was not so much the rain or wind; we got a good dose of that with the near constant trade winds. The problem was the *direction* of all the rain and wind – Kona storms approached from the opposite direction of the trade winds. They came from the south.

Opposite of the trade winds was something that only happened maybe a couple of times a decade. Buildings, restaurants, hotel lobbies, and Tiwaka's Tiki Bar & Grill were all constructed for trade winds, keeping their walls oriented to the northeast and the open lanais, sitting areas and furniture exposed to the west and south, aiming for the sunsets. Kona storms came in from the south or southwest toward everyone's unprotected areas. The islands could always expect a good soaking when one showed up. They were for the most part locally generated tropical depressions. They would form in the warmer waters several hundred miles south and drift up to where we were, usually to wither and die between our massive volcanic peaks and cooler waters.

Sandy, Ma and Pa and I were busy picking up chairs and putting the ones with cushions in the shed while those without only got a ceremonial look. After that was done, I pulled down my blue tarp barrier to protect the wall of liqueur bottles. Tiwaka's perch between the vodka bottles sat empty.

"Has anyone seen Tiwaka yet?" I turned and asked.

Everyone looked at me and silently shook their heads. Pa looked up to the rain clouds piling up just uphill of us and shook his head.

"Bad day to be flying."

"Pa!" Ma whispered. "We know that already."

Pa shook his head and went back to moving chairs.

"I know, just saying ..."

I walked out from behind the bar and took a good look up into the sky. A light rain was blowing all through the area, soaking my upturned face in a matter of moments. There were certainly no birds flying. Nothing up there but gray and my dread.

Sandy walked up to me, putting her hand on my shoulder. "Maybe Wailani would know something?"

I kissed her forehead a little to thank her for the distraction, and the idea.

"If I hadn't thought I saw him going up into that cloud I would just think he was out eating bugs ..." My voice cracked a bit. "You know ..." I tried to continue. "... bugs come up from the ground when it rains ..."

The rain was just a drizzle but I could hear the large trees behind me in the jungle dropping big drops of water they had held as long as they could.

"He'll be just fine babe," Sandy reassured. "Remember, he's had a long history of good things happening to him."

I knew she didn't want to say he was "lucky" or "nothing ever happens to good people and/or parrots". She was being analytical, God bless her! If history was any guide, she was hinting, his ability to stay out of trouble would most likely continue.

"Wailani should be here soon," Sandy said squeezing me again. "You know she's got a good read on these kinds of things."

A low booming roll of thunder started up near the summit of Haleakala just then, and began falling through the valleys, bouncing off the vertical walls, cascading up and over the trees and finally surrounding all of us at the bar. It was vibrating right through our chests!

A bolt of lightning shot through the air, from one end of the sky to the other chasing us inside. I think it chased quite a bit of confidence from me as well. Standing under the roof of the bar we all looked out to the sheets of rain now pouring from the sky. It was looking ... I stopped that thought and closed my eyes for a moment to concentrate.

I wasn't completely helpless toward my friend Tiwaka. My hands and feet might not be able to help him, but I did have one tool left. Trying to focus on his situation, caught up in storm clouds full of lightning and pounding rain, I thought how I might handle such a situation. Taking that thought I then focused as much as my feeble mind would allow and reached out to him in my imagination.

"Tiwaka," I said silently in my mind, then took a slow deep breath. "Tiwaka!" I called, flexing every muscle in my body, clenching my fists tightly. "Roll with the punches dude."

~~~

Tiwaka now realized missing breakfast was working to his advantage. With all the rolling and spinning he would have thrown it up anyhow.

The bright flashes of lightning were scaring him especially since the thunder vibrated through his body as intensely as the light stung his eyes. The heavy movements of wind had forced him to fold his wings in, but when they abruptly stopped he began falling again and tried to fly.

Flying was not quite the correct word; it was more like slowing an inevitable crash. Flapping his sore wings after he fell for what felt like a minute or two, another violent column of heavy pulsing air carried him up again.

His bird navigation sense told him he must be far from Haleakala and the bar by this point. Yet, he felt it must be mistaken, confused by the storm, since he felt he must be many miles away, out over the water. One thing he did know for sure was that he was moving west northwest.

The other confusing part was why he continued to get colder and colder. He wasn't sure how high he might be, he remembered encountering chilly air on his first day of flying. Inside that small part of his mind where he wasn't terrified he smiled a brief moment thinking of his first day of flying. It was as if it were only yesterday! As another violent updraft propelled him into colder and colder air he laughed a bit. It *had* been only yesterday!

~~~

I was tossing my tenth or fifteen bucket of muddy water from the bar floor out into the jungle as Wailani rounded the corner of the muddy driveway. She was soaking wet, her waist length jet black hair hugging her like a blanket.

As soon as she saw me at the edge of the jungle she ran up to me and grabbed my hands.

"Is Tiwaka here?" she asked worriedly. Her large watery brown eyes were betraying her. I think she was too upset to worry about that and felt comfortable around me anyhow.

I looked up at her, trying to hold back my emotions, thankful that the rain running down my face would hide any tears that insisted on flowing.

"No, he's...."

Wailani looked immediately up into the clouds, squeezing my hands tightly.

"He's up there? Flying?"

My eyebrows knitted together and I shook my head sideways.

"I think so Wailani," the rain now doing a great job of hiding things. "I think I saw him go up ... into the clouds ..."

Great thunder rocked the ground beneath us, forcing us to run back inside the bar. Both of us just looked at each other, not bothering to dry off. I was taking advantage of my rain streaked face mask a lot now.

"Can I have some time off then?" Wailani asked.

I shrugged my shoulders and murmured, "Of course."

"I can look for him, you know. My friends and I."

My eyes picked themselves up out of despair and found hers, large and watery and reminding me of Coco again. She was smiling slightly. If I hadn't been in such a state of grief, knowing it can cloud one's thoughts and perceptions, I would swear there was a bit of a glow around her.

"Your friends?" I asked. As I asked I immediately found the answer.

She nodded and winked lightly, smiling again.

Of course, I thought, her friends in the sea.

Reaching forward to hug her I couldn't help but say "It's good to have friends in the sea when you live on an island, eh?"

~~~

It seemed to have been hours now since Tiwaka had visited Ococ at his old grave. The violent updrafts had been fewer and farther between now giving the parrot a chance to glide through the thick mists between the boiling clouds.

"Ococ," Tiwaka managed to say lightly, his first words since jumping off the bamboo cross. His wings were fully extended and he could see significant tears in his outer feathers. Delicately he flapped his wings a bit to test his muscles. They were sore but they were working.

"Ococ, where am I?" Tiwaka thought to himself. His beak seemed a bit stiff, until he wiggled it enough to force a chunk of ice away.

Loud booming thunder was just behind and above him and ahead was another dark wall of cloud. Below him looked lighter, but still obscured and straight up looked … a lightning bolt streaked across just then.

The wind here was still calm giving Tiwaka a few moments to think, instead of having to react blow by blow to another beating. Thunder was trouble, so were the dark clouds. Below looked less threatening. Surely he would find a place to rest there, perhaps a piece of ground in which to burrow and escape the weather.

He took a deep breath and shook his feet a little, flapped his wings and continued to glide, rising slightly with the wind. For a moment he opened his mind, like he had on the cross, and tried to find something, anything that might give him a clue as to what to do. He was tired, hungry and afraid that if he got caught in another series of updrafts he might lose the little control he had been able to maintain. He might even fall into unconsciousness and not be able to stop himself in a fall.

It seemed, Tiwaka figured, the best path was lower. It was away from the thunder and lightning and not directly into the dark cloud wall far ahead. By habit or by design he turned his head, looking below him first with his left eye, and then turning the other direction to scan it with his right. He could ascertain neither true intentions nor dreams and so with that he folded his wings slightly and began a steep descent lower.

It felt good to be flying again, under his own power as it were. The wind caressed his tiny face feathers gently and whisked away much of the water that he had been carrying. He took a moment to close his eyes, and truly relax a moment. Wild eyed terror had forced them open since he had been sucked up into that first cloud base. Now, with another deep breath, he opened his mind widely, looking for Ococ.

It felt really good to relax. In fact gliding and descending was actually rejuvenating him, and he was feeling a little stronger with the rest. His eyes were just too comfortable to open quite yet, but he did peek briefly. Same scene, gray mists, lighter below, darker above and far ahead.

With any luck there would be a nice bug filled tree below, with beautiful Mynah birds awaiting his every beck and call. Small little Finches would trim his rough talons, and pick off any parasites from every feather. Pigeons would bring him overripe berries fermented by the wise Owls. And Peacocks, oh those Peacocks … they would allow him to sit among them for hours upon hours.

"Ococ," Tiwaka mused. "It will be so nice."

He heard nothing in response. Peeking once more he saw nothing changed and closed his eyes again. Feeling he must try to contact Ococ he opened his soul fully, clearing his mind of everything.

The air was thickening, feeling so much more like home.

"Ococ," Tiwaka tried again. "What should I do?"

This time Tiwaka did feel Ococ touch him inside, in his mind. His dog growl was less cheerful this time, in fact it seemed a bit urgent.

"What is it Ococ? What should I do?" Tiwaka asked lightly, feeling his wings grip the air so much easier now, smelling the thick tropical air once again. The sounds from Ococ were increasingly insistent now and it wasn't until Tiwaka opened his eyes that he knew why.

"Fly Tiwaka! Fly!" Ococ's voice said.

Salt spray from a wild frothy ocean reached up from only a few dozen feet below to coat his feathers in a mist of brine. Immediately he flapped powerfully, trying to pull higher, but not before another splash of ocean nipped at his tail feathers and his talons.

"Fly!" Tiwaka now chanted in terror. "Fly!" In a moment he had checked his suicide descent into the sea and leveled off at fifty feet. Looking around he saw a dark gray mass of confused ocean mixed with bursts of white water, in all directions. Above him the cloud deck waited, frothing itself in a reflective dance with the sea.

Quickly, Tiwaka did a full circling turn to try and get his bearings. He almost had a fix but lightning behind him confused his attempt, so he tried again. As he completed that turn he finally understood it didn't really matter which way he was flying. Behind him, or at least in the direction he had come, massive lightning bolts were streaking through the sky, followed by thunder that might crush his bird bones with their sonic volume. Ahead and slightly to the left was another dark wall cloud extending practically down to the water. Below was a bigger danger, if he got into the water he would surely drown.

Sea turtles were popping up for air and a brief thought entered his mind: if only the seas were calmer he could land on their shell and rest. That though was clearly impossible.

Ahead and to the right seemed the only viable option. And, to climb. He must climb up and away from the ocean; altitude would give him time to react to a fall. Altitude was the savior of all fliers.

He started to climb higher and began entering the misty cloud base again, fearful of what he knew was there - more updrafts that would beat him, more rain that would soak him, more ice that might weigh him down. The sea would surely kill him, but in the air he at least had a chance.

Tiwaka moved higher and higher now, into the thickening mists of the clouds. He had to climb higher, embracing altitude. He flew up, to where the monsters lived.

~~~

Ma & Pa had retired to their home near the cliffs while Sandy sat in the tree house with Baby Kiawe. Wailani had left on her mission to find out some information about Tiwaka.

I had just returned from Unknowns chasing some crazy idea that Tiwaka might have been forced to land in the bay and was trying to swim in. Of course, if he had, there would have been no swimming to be had. The brown water was churning so violently from the choppy surf and swirling winds that nothing short of a submarine could survive.

It had taken me a full thirty minutes to pull myself back up the muddy stream that had been the trail when I had gone down it. Flash floods were not to be tested in these parts of Maui, so I had taken to the edges of the jungle, pulling myself uphill along vines and tree trunks. My slippers had long ago entered the bay no doubt.

I kept my eyes peeled for any flashes of color in the jungle that might point to a downed parrot. The only thing I saw that came close were hundreds of ripe yellow guavas rolling downhill with the muddy water.

"Poor Tiwaka's gonna miss all those treats," I said to myself. I was already to the point of making jokes to manage my grief. It was an old standby for pain, but I knew it wouldn't help my friend. Sandy, Shiloh, Coco, Ma & Pa and even Wailani had proven to me time and time again that mental attitude, optimism, and positive thinking would save the day. I knew they were right.

Still, I thought the cascading guavas were funny. Reaching down to catch one, but missing and then trying again successfully, I put two delicately into my pocket.

Tiwaka would appreciate it when we found him.

~~~

Spend several hours in a war zone and you eventually learn a few survival skills. Tiwaka was quickly picking up cues from the storm as to which clouds would kick his butt and which might lift him higher.

The lightning though seemed to be everywhere. When it flashed he found if he closed his eyes immediately after he could see a detailed image of what lay ahead. The grayness of the clouds masked almost everything, but the flashes of bright light painted shadows and textures that gave him navigation options, or not.

It wasn't long before he found himself surrounded again with bad routes. Thunder was moving over him and coming up behind him as well. Lightning had even streaked below him a few times. Ahead, illuminated with a series of long lightning flashes was a wall of boiling rising cloud.

He tried to steer right, hoping to go around most of it. That wasn't to be. In a moment, as if from behind, he was quickly accelerated into the cloud wall, slamming into a rushing of air that tumbled, beat and carried him violently aloft.

Tucking his wings in tightly and closing his eyes he rolled with the punches, bravely accepting whatever it was the storm was intent on giving him.

Tiwaka along with most tropical birds are a tough crowd, even in captivity. They can live for decades, eat most anything and survive most hazards, natural or manmade.

Electricity though wasn't something they were designed to withstand. Of course, they have the same miniscule currents of it coursing through their nerve fibers just like we do. Their brains rely on minute electrical signals as well. Muscles flex and relax based on electrical signals.

However, the electricity found in thunderstorms can be quite destructive to organic life forms. If the raw energy of a lightning strike doesn't completely cook you, just a little glance of it can scramble your own internal electrical grid, stopping your heart or prompting seizures in your brain.

Tiwaka could feel the heat now from some of the bolts rocketing past his tumbling half frozen body. He had decided to keep his eyes closed, at least until he felt a falling sensation again. Of course he had only felt a rising sensation for a very long time, and the frigid temperature was starting to scare him.

He tried to flex his talons but found they wouldn't respond. Opening his wings might get them ripped right off his body. Turning his head slightly, that should be something he could do.

He could not.

Half frozen, covered in a thin sheet of ice, Tiwaka was becoming a large piece of hail, rocketing up to the highest reaches of the cumulus beast at the heart of this thunderstorm.

Unable to turn his head he tried opening his eyes. It took a couple of tries but he managed to break through the thin ice there by blinking rapidly. He seemed to still be, impossibly so, rising higher. All of the thunder was below him now. Lightning was close but it too seemed to be falling below him as he climbed higher within the powerful updraft.

It seemed dark above him, but not cloud dark. It appeared to be early evening dark. The cloud was thinning in the direction he was going!

Another powerful thunderclap seemed to literally push him from below with a sonic wave and indeed in a second he was actually free of the cloud.

High up in the clear dry air! He tried to open his wings, but they weren't responding. He wiggled his talons as hard as he could, but nothing worked. Amazingly he was still climbing, along with hundreds of pieces of hail, all propelled out of the top of the thunderstorm along with him.

In just a moment his ascent slowed and he felt he might begin falling again, this time frozen and unable to fly. Several pieces of hail were already falling back, but his own extra momentum carried him higher for another few seconds.

Looking below he could see lightning flashing inside the cloud and rising, rising up and striking the falling hail chunks. It looked like a snake striking out at rats in a cage, tiny bolts of electricity tagging each piece of ice as they fell lower.

Tiwaka struggled to open his wings as he reached his peak, tumbled once over and began to fall, slowly at first. It was then that the lightning struck several pieces of rising hail moving past him to their peak. Tiny bolts were reaching out from the cloud top into the clear air, striking and bursting each into a shower of tiny sparkling pieces. Each piece was getting hit and finally he saw it coming for him. After all this, was he going to be struck dead once clear of the storm?

As he tumbled over again and his view of the cloud was blocked he saw an island below, a few miles to the side. Its mountains were free of the storm, its edges were decorated in bright lights! The deep blues of late sunset and early evening were just beyond its shores to the west.

"It's beautiful…" he thought, just as he was hit. The tiny lightning bolt reached out and tagged his ice covered body, shattering his cage and freeing his wings. It hurt intensely for just a moment. After that he felt a tingle, an uncontrollable shudder move through every part of his body. He felt it crawl right into his mind, feeling its way around, exploring and pushing through his rapidly fading consciousness.

Tiwaka couldn't see it himself, now falling unconscious from twenty thousand feet, but a glow seemed to envelope him for a few moments as the electricity played amongst his feathers, his hollow bones and inside his head.

From just below his falling body, looking up, one could see the storm showering the deep blues of space with thousands of pieces of white hail, throwing them high and out over the falling parrot. Lightning was striking most of them, one or two at a time. It might have reminded one of a celebratory water cannon salute embedded with a fireworks show.

As he continued to fall, still unconscious, Tiwaka dreamed. His mind raced rapidly, soaking up a rich mix of wonder and fascination. He could see everyone at the bar, worried about him; he could hear the sea turtles talking about him almost crashing into the waves. He could see Ococ and Coco smiling at him with incredibly happy faces. They seemed to be dancing and singing a little song.

"Fly, Tiwaka, open your wings, and fly again." It took him a moment or two to get beyond the enjoyment of seeing them dance together and figure out the meaning of their words.

At fifteen thousand feet Tiwaka shook it off, woke up, found his wings and flexed them into full glider mode. He felt horrible, bruised and kicked but the beautiful island of lights was at the bottom of his projected path. He looked back and up, saw the storm retreating behind him and the shower of hail mingling with the first stars of twilight.

Turning back to continue aiming for the island below, he shook off the pain, and sucked in a nice clean breath of air. An overwhelming sense of jubilation coursed through every sore muscle, every feather! It was good to be alive!

From a distance the fountain of hail and tiny lightning was quite beautiful. Dozens of sailboats, catamarans and a lone schooner far below marveled at the spectacle. People all over the warm beaches there, some still swimming in the luxurious waters, felt fortunate to be able to watch.

Tiwaka didn't know it of course, but the storm was indeed celebrating his adventure *and* his escape. Few who flew within its heart did both, and those that had, they moved differently among the rest of us. Second chances are the ultimate transformative experience, not just for the survivor but for all they touch later.

~~~

Honolulu City Lights

Captain T.R. Wheeler clicked off the autopilot and manually guided his Hawaiian Airlines Boeing 767-300ER far clear of the heavy weather just southeast of the Honolulu International Airport. Banking left and lowering the nose for their downwind approach to runway 08L both he, the co-pilot and the jumpseater watched as the huge flight deck windows filled with the lights of Waikiki.

"That cell seems stationary where it is," the co-pilot remarked, watching his onboard weather radar closely for movement. Such a large thunderstorm cell could create a micro burst right above a runway, making landing a risky maneuver.

"Strange how the front stalled right there," Captain Wheeler noted. "Must be quite a show from the beach."

"A show I hope to soon be enjoying at the Shorebird," the co-pilot practically sang. "Ten days off in Waikiki, I must be living right!"

Honolulu Tower was on the cockpit speakers, as well as their headphones. "Temperature seven eight, winds calm zero eight zero at zero two. Altimeter two niner seven four."

"I don't like the wind being that still, it's like the calm before the storm, it could swing either way at the last moment," the co-pilot whispered to himself. He looked up from his instruments to scan the sky ahead.

"Hey, is that a balloon?" he announced, pointing. "Eleven o'clock, high."

Captain Wheeler tightened his grip reflexively on the yoke, while looking out. What he saw couldn't have been a balloon.

"It's descending, can't be a balloon...maybe it's..."

"Holy...it's a bird?" The co-pilot interjected, checking his altimeter. "At eight thousand feet?"

Captain Wheeler projected the path of the falling object and extended his turning descent to give whatever it was plenty of room.

"Tower, Hawaiian twenty-nine, are you showing any traffic, balloons maybe, at eight thousand?" The co-pilot asked. "We're seeing something relatively large descending at our one o'clock position, maybe seventy-five hundred now."

A moment of silence passed on the radio as all three on the flight deck tried to make out the identity of the UFO.

"Negative Hawaiian twenty-nine," Tower responded. The controller though had seen a lot of strange things in his almost thirty year experience and added, "Could be ice falls from the cell to your right."

"Roger Tower," the co-pilot acknowledged. "We have the airport in sight."

The massive Boeing 767 was moving at two hundred and thirty knots, descending at eight hundred feet per minute, carving out a graceful arch just offshore of Diamond Head. The object was coming up quickly off their right wing now.

"Do you think it's a bird Captain?"

"Looks like a hawk or an eagle, the way it's diving like that," Captain Wheeler answered. "I don't know, I thought we didn't have those types of birds out here...wait..."

At their closest pass to the object all three of them recognized what it was, but were so dumbfounded no one spoke for a second or two.

"A parrot? Was that a parrot?" the co-pilot finally asked, looking to his altimeter again. "At six thousand feet?"

Captain Wheeler was keying his mic to inform the tower. "Tower, we identified our traffic as a bird. A large Macaw actually, descending rapidly toward Waikiki."

"Roger Hawaiian twenty-nine, we aren't painting anything here. Confirm traffic no longer a factor?"

The co-pilot gave Captain Wheeler a thumbs up as he watched the bird descend well below them and to their right now, heading for the bright lights.

"Hawaiian twenty-nine clear."

"Roger Hawaiian twenty-nine," the Tower answered. "Clear to land runway eight left, wind zero niner zero at fifteen. Be advised, Aloha Cargo experienced a wind-shear +/- 10 to 15 knots at 100 feet 5 minutes ago."

Things began getting real busy as the crew prepared for a surprise change in the wind at landing, but the co-pilot couldn't help but ask.

"Captain, how did you recognize that as a macaw?"

"Saw one in a Tiki bar on Maui once. Flaps twenty, gear down, landing check." Captain Wheeler reached up to turn on the nose gear lights. "Maybe he's headed to a Tiki bar now."

"Flaps twenty, three green Captain," the co-pilot followed. "Maybe I'll see him later tonight!"

Captain Wheeler took another good scan of his instruments, looked over at his co-pilot and commented, "Anything's possible!"

~~~

The Good Ship Tiki

Tiwaka felt the air thickening quickly, buffeting his battered body so much that he had to slow down. Pulling up slightly from his dive he could feel the strain in his wings and neck. Pain was radiating all through his muscles reminding him that his adventure wouldn't quite end until he could rest somewhere.

As he got closer and closer to the brilliantly decorated strip of beach and buildings he saw that his glide would not take him all the way there. In fact, at this rate he would land somewhere in the rolling surf, if he didn't collide with any of the dozens of stand-up paddlers.

Of course, he could try and flap his wings a bit and make the extra few hundred feet, but he was increasingly sore. And he felt as if he might get sick any moment. Exhaustion was his motivator, his master, and if he didn't land soon, his executioner.

He tried circling once in his glide now, looking below to see what options there might be. His left eye was cloudy from dust or ice or whatever, but his right eye, the one that could discern dreams, was clear.

There, just below, on a slow tack west, was a two masted schooner, out by itself beyond the crowd of catamarans, party boats and surfers. There didn't seem to be anyone on board that he could see. It would have to do.

Tiwaka circled three more times, descending rapidly despite his attempts to slow it down. He took a final turn and glided in toward the schooner from the stern. At this point he was committed to making this landing, this boat. Any mistakes he knew would be unrecoverable, his energy just about spent.

Approaching too fast he tried braking several feet away, flaring his wings and dropping his tail and talons. That seemed to work well, allowing him to read the escutcheon as he glided over.

Unfortunately, what he saw demanded a surprised chuckle, causing him to miss the railing and slam firmly into the helm. That in turn released a rope tied with an small bell setting it to sing out. Bouncing down to the deck, Tiwaka ended up knocking over a large mason glass filled with something vaguely familiar. A booming voice sounded from below.

"Who's there?"

Adrenaline his only power source now Tiwaka scrambled back up to the top of the escutcheon and peered over to read the name again. Incredible! How perfect he thought, looking back to mid ships for the voice - no one was coming yet. He looked over the side again, incredulous,

Honolulu

"What's all the racket?"

A tall and comfortably dark, unusually handsome shirtless man came back to the helm. He appeared to be smiling despite the interruption. A tiki amulet hung from a leather strap around his neck.

Tiwaka sat very still on the chair behind the helm, wondering if this guy would throw him overboard. Being quiet was going to be impossible, as the decompression from his descent had worked up quite a loud burp. He had to let it go or burst!

"Well!" the sailor looked over at Tiwaka and began laughing. "You're in fine shape aren't you?" He walked over and sat down next to Tiwaka. "Did you drink my entire drink or spill all of it?"

Before Tiwaka could answer he added, "Careful how you answer bird ... spilling it all could get you a long walk on a short plank!"

He reached over to lightly pet the tousled feathers, inspecting the beat up bird. "My guess is that you must have drunk it, by the looks of you." His hands went to Tiwaka's back, attempting to stroke the tattered feathers back into place. "You're cold! How..."

Standing up he walked back out of sight for just a moment and returned quickly with a wool sweater. "Here, let me wrap this around you, if you don't mind my friend."

Tiwaka took the offering with a small squawk. It was about all he could offer at this point.

"How might you have gotten so cold?"

Tiwaka tried to turn and look up and over to the storm clouds still parked southeast of Honolulu. His new sailor friend glanced that way too, watched the lightning pop off a few and then looked back to the parrot.

"Yeah," he whispered, looking away. "I was that cold for a while, but hey!" Standing up and waving his arms, "Here I am now! Warm and happy!" Sitting back down his grin dominated his youthful face. It was one of those smiles that forced you to quickly close the screen door less it invade your very soul with an overwhelming confidence. He adjusted the wool sweater a little tighter around his feathered shipmate. "And, it looks as if I have a new friend!" He sat there smiling for just a moment before adding, "Welcome aboard the *Tiki!*"

Tiwaka looked at the man closely, first with his now working left eye, for his true intentions. He appeared genuine if not a touch overly happy. Turning his head to look at him with his right eye, to read his dreams, Tiwaka got a small jolt straight to his weakened heart. No! It couldn't be, Tiwaka thought. He looked around at the schooner, the sails, the ropes, the deck. They had it too, a slight glow, just like the man did. Not much of a glow but it was there, shimmering. Maybe, Tiwaka thought, it could be his vision still in disrepair from the battering he had just survived.

The man held out his hand for Tiwaka to shake.

"What shall I call you my fine feathered bird friend?"

Tiwaka was still overwhelmed by it all. The battering in the storm, the last moment crash landing on a boat named *Tiki* and now it looked like he might be dreaming it all!

"Tiwaka!" the exhausted bird answered, staring at the sailor. It was all finally too much and he fell, dead asleep, into the kind man's hand.

"Well then, Tiwaka..." He picked up the bird, and carried him down to the cabin where he placed him on some pillows. "You rest for a while matey. We're headed to port, perhaps a place you might like."

He paused to light a cigarette. "Oldest Tiki bar on the island I've been told, and I must admit one of my all time favorite places." He placed a small bowl of water close by and found some cashews to set next to that.

"Of course, I've got a free slip there, so I'm partial."

He climbed the ladder back up to the deck and headed to the stern. The last of the evening colors were just about spent. That storm off to the southeast had remained parked and thus had quelled the usually rambunctious trade winds down to a whisper.

"Miss Suzi," he said loudly in case the parrot could actually hear him. "She can take good care of you, Mister Tiwaka. You won't be the first parrot to be rescued by her capable hands."

He steered his silent schooner past several smaller boats all making their way toward Waikiki. Despite his expert maneuvering, they all came dangerously close, acting as if they didn't even see the *Tiki*. *Tiki* was headed in the opposite direction toward Sand Island, the next harbor over from Honolulu and a particular stand of tall coconut palms marking the entrance to the marina there.

"Oh, Mister Tiwaka, sorry ol' boy, but I forgot to introduce myself!" He spun the helm twenty degrees to port and then stood off to the side, holding it firmly with one hand.

Looking for the entrance through the reef just ahead he announced loudly, to Tiwaka and to anyone else predisposed to listen, "Gardner McKay at your service and we are going to La Mariana for cocktails!"

~~~

La Mariana Sailing Club

The light chop of the sea tapped out a melody to the sleeping parrot below decks. Tiwaka must have been asleep for at least half an hour when the smell of fresh water and nuts drifted down to his nose, stirring him from sleep.

He sat up as best he could wrapped in the wool, but he was too bound to move well. Taking several minutes of wing flexing and rolling around on the floor he eventually freed himself of it and quickly made his way to the table top.

Despite the fact that the nuts had been neglected when chocolate was being distributed, they still tasted heavenly. The water was gone quickly as well. Somewhat invigorated he made his way up the ladder to the open deck.

The sky was littered with bright stars interrupted occasionally by a jetliner taking off from the nearby Honolulu International. A light breeze had picked up moving them along nicely through the reef opening and toward the line of tiki torches ashore.

"Aye, Mister Tiwaka!" Gardner shouted from the stern. "Watch the bow for me, will you?"

Tiwaka wondered what he might be looking for that would require an alert. The water here was plenty deep as well as calm as they approached the marina docks.

"Turtles, you know! They sometimes forget about the boats." Gardner spun the helm a full two spins, bringing the eight-five foot schooner perfectly alongside a much newer sixty foot racer.

"Nice, eh?" Gardner asked Tiwaka, nodding to the sleek composite marvel. "Racing boats these days are rocket ships…" Tying off a quick line to the racer and then running to the bow to tie one more he laughed. "These guys don't mind me borrowing their port side for a few hours I'll bet."

Sure enough Tiwaka spotted several green sea turtles frolicking in a small patch of seaweed between the tied up boats. Two of them took a long moment to look at him, and then went back to playing. He looked toward the dozens of tiki torches along the dock leading up to the others by the restaurant and bar. Despite there being twenty or so boats tied up there seemed to be no one around.

"Come ashore Tiwaka, they've got a Lychee Martini that will make you sing like Pavarotti!" Gardner silently glided up and over *Tiki's* railing, landing on the racing sloop's deck without a sound. He turned to look for Tiwaka.

"Are you coming?"

Tiwaka tried to hobble over to the railing, a huge effort in itself, but couldn't make the short leap up to the railing. Gardner glided just as silently back over to *Tiki's* deck.

"You are a bit of a mess aren't you? No worries, let me carry you in, if you don't mind?"

Tiwaka managed to finally say something. "Mahalo…" It sounded more like a squeak than a thank you.

Gardner stopped in his tracks and looked at the tattered parrot he now held on his arm, steadying it with his other hand.

"How many words do you know?"

Tiwaka nodded his head and found enough energy to belt out a nice loud "Aloha!"

Gardner laughed uproariously. "No kidding! Aloha right back at you Tiwaka!"

In only a moment they seemed to be on the dock making their way toward the silent restaurant and Tiki bar. Gardner hoisted Tiwaka up onto his shoulder and marched like the King himself straight inside and directly to the bar.

Tiwaka had to duck under several low hanging puffer fish lights and several strings of Christmas lights but otherwise enjoyed the ride. At first glance there seemed to be only a couple of tables in the back with one or two people, and no one at the bar except an old gray surfer type. Tiwaka was still taking in all the décor when suddenly Gardner burst into song.

"Just sit right back and you'll hear a tale,
a tale of a fateful trip.
That started from this tropic port,
aboard this tiny ship."

Just as suddenly Tiwaka noticed an immediate change in the bar area. All the hanging fishing balls lit up, blue, red and yellow. A small crowd materialized where he *thought* there had been no one...he blinked a few times, but there they were. Everyone was laughing and talking loudly. Colorful highly decorated drinks were in everyone's hands and soon a martini showed up in Gardner's.

"Here's to your health Tiwaka!" Gardner saluted. He leaned in close to Tiwaka's ear and whispered. "You can have the lychee later."

This party looked like it was going to quickly gear up to mach one. Four or five good looking local ladies walked in with their ukuleles. It was five, Tiwaka thought, five for sure.

The bartender, who now looked to be in his late twenties, seemed to be the center of attention for the most part. His mixology was drawing a gathering. This was a young crowd, Tiwaka suddenly noticed, not a gray hair in the joint!

"Hey, meet my new shipmate," Gardner was announcing to a circle of friends. "Tiwaka, from distant parts unknown."

They all lifted their drinks and nodded. The lovely lady amongst the men smiled softly.

"Here Tiwaka, this is Mister Ho," Gardner began.

"Ah, Tiwaka," Gardner's friend corrected. "Just call me Don."

"Aloooha!" Tiwaka said with some authority. "Mister Aloha!" he added.

"We've got another Donn over here Tiwaka," Gardner said turning slightly. "Beachcomber that he is, he can't sing anywhere near as well."

"What you drinking, Tiwaka?" Donn asked. "I recommend something I like to call a Mai Tai." He leaned in a little closer. "Have you heard of it?"

Tiwaka wasn't the best historian, but he did know that the Mai Tai had been around longer than he had. Yet here was a guy acting like it was something new.

"Yes. Yes I have," Tiwaka nodded, whispering to himself, almost loud enough to be heard.

"See!" Donn said to his circle of friends. "They still talk about it!"

Could this really be the Don *and* the Donn? Was this all some hail-up-side-the-head induced hallucination? Tiwaka felt a kernel of reality buried deep in his consciousness, saying this couldn't be real. Yet that kernel was only willing to stay quiet and observe everything else that was happening. In that case, he would just go with the flow.

The sultry looking lady was watching Tiwaka closer than he himself might an unguarded macadamia nut wrapped in a half melted layer of fine milk chocolate. Gardner turned to her next, of course. He went to introduce her but she quickly interrupted.

"Vicky," her gaze considered his disheveled look against his natural parrot handsomeness. "Would you like to do the Violet Jive with me?"

Tiwaka wasn't sure if her beautifully full red lips were puckering for him or his ride. He looked over to Gardner and saw him politely smiling.

"Tiwaka here just dropped in and could use a good night's rest. He is also my personal guest for however many days it takes to ..." Gardner turned to look at his colorful shipmate and brushed his head feathers "... to get his mojo back."

"Mojo!" everyone chimed in with a tip of their Mai Tai, Zombie, Samoan Fog Cutter, Blue Hawaii, Singapore Sling or sparkling Mauna Kea seltzer.

Tiwaka immediately reached into Gardner's drink and grabbed the lychee floating on top. A quick flick of the neck and it disappeared inside his beak.

"Mojo!" Gardner saluted again.

"Mojo baby!" Tiwaka managed to repeat as his head started to spin.

~~~

All You Need

It hadn't stopped raining and I had already searched the most likely spots. If Tiwaka had any chance to make it back, to turn all this into just a memorable story to be told around campfires, he would be at the bay, somewhere along the long winding gravel driveway or near the tool shed. Maybe I would find him up on Hana Highway's less than consistent two lanes of black asphalt, or luxuriating inside one of the dozen or so abandoned surf cars, or even exploring a bored garbage can for tasty bugs.

Before my flashlight finally broke, on the third drop, I had searched half way to Paia town. My iPhone flashlight took over after that, but when dawn arrived I still had no leads.

After a to-go quart of organically nurtured, fair trade, Mozart serenaded, hippie grown coffee and a ketchup hot dog from next door at the gas station I made my way west.

Nothing was to be found at the airport or the beaches just on the other side of the runway. The sand dunes held nothing that might be construed as a parrot, but did harbor quite a few campers, teenagers and stoners. Crowds were good though. Crowds would help in a search since Tiwaka would no doubt be the center of attention, drawing throngs of people like a magnet would iron shavings. But, there was nothing here.

Kahului and Wailuku and neighboring Iao Valley held only mud, leaf strewn sidewalks and people under umbrellas. Turning south and traversing miles of flat sugar cane fields, I plodded the beaches between Ma'alaea and Makena, some twenty miles or so. Nothing again but murky water where the sharks owned the surf for the next few days.

The sun set on me in the lava fields of La Perouse Bay and I slept in a pocket of sand I found near the water. At first light I began again.

The pali road, on the way to Lahaina, was peppered with smaller rocks that had made it through the cliff's boulder fences during the storm, forcing everyone to slow and weave their way along. The tunnel was spilling water over its edges like a car wash greets a paying customer.

Front street was busy with shop owners trying to prepare for the cruise ship's arrival in an hour. The two thousand passenger mega bar had ridden out the weather far to the east. It would be an excellent day of shopping since none of the tourists would bother with a guided tour or outdoor adventure of any kind. Broken awnings and garbage were being hauled off in pickup trucks by family enlisted for cleanup. There was nothing here either.

Ka'anapali held little for a parrot searcher, nor the rising coffee plantations above Kapalua. The wind had returned back to brisk trades, full of moisture and vigor and intent on pushing me back home. It wanted me to grieve on my own side of the island.

I stopped the truck on the side of the road overlooking Honolua Bay, settling two tires in puddles deep enough to muddy my rims. Rain was still misting heavily as it tried to hide the green cliffs of Molokai across the channel. Dark cobalt laced seas dared anyone to cross, by boat or wing. Foreboding as it did appear, Molokai and her surrounding ocean carpet always seemed to promise me something. Today was no different. Its waterfalls and cliffs were silently calling in a deep jungle octave, something only my heart could hear. One day, I knew I would understand whatever message it was. Apparently it was not today.

I scanned her coastline from the near cliffs left toward the desert west end and just over the horizon, to where O'ahu would be. Honolulu was probably sixty or so miles from here. The storm had traveled that direction, before falling apart.

With all those places to safely land perhaps Tiwaka might have made it to safety on either island. I walked over to a large boulder, brushed away as much water as I could and sat down with my knees under my elbows, my arms crossed and holding my chin. I stared west along the arch of the Hawaiian Islands. The perspective was one of massive extremes, large islands nearly submersed by an almost infinitely deep sea, and all of this covered by an even larger blanket of atmosphere above. Tiwaka was so tiny in all that, so inconsequential.

The wind gusted again, moving deliberately between the channel and into the bay, rubbing my hair like a proud uncle. I was so infinitesimal in all of this as well. How was I going to find him?

I've never had to knock on wood, but I know people who have. Now, I was beginning to understand why they did. It didn't feel like something one might do when faced with overwhelming odds, gambling against almost certain failure. No, not at all actually. It felt like the powers at hand - nature in its largess of scale and its depth of compassion, only required a request. A knock. A sign that you understood that hope existed.

I could hear someone telling me a little secret, the wind or an angel; it was often difficult for me to discern the difference. "Ask for what you need, ask it of the greatness there before you." This phrase repeated itself to me as I looked out to sea, lightly repeating with every breath of wind. It was a chant I had heard often while sitting quiet amidst the majestic vistas of Hawaii.

Asking was always a little difficult for me. It felt like an admission of weakness, a guy thing I guess. Despite that emotion I had enough sense to listen to good advice.

I watched the sea dancing with the wind another minute. A fishing boat was making its way downwind. Fishermen are a faithful bunch as I remember. Old man Tedeshi used to tell us kids on the docks that he dreamed of big catches of Ahi. Not every night, but when he did he made for the deep waters and sure enough he found them. If dreaming was asking for what you want, then I was good to go.

The impressive scale of the mountains, the deep oceans and impervious air seemed matched only by our own amazing capacity to ask - with a knock on wood or a dream.

Those supplications must then focus this impressive spirit of nature into our own minds. From there we might call forth our heartfelt wishes.

I had seen others do it, had no doubt benefited from the practice by others, especially my parents, and now for the first time in my life understood how and why people did so...

... The sun moved out from behind low gray clouds for the briefest of moments. My eyes felt the gaze of the universe and for the first time in my life I prayed.

~~~

Shorthanded

Three days had now passed and there was still no sign of Tiwaka. The bar was unusually somber. In fact once word had gotten out through the coconut wireless, Twitter and Facebook, our usual crowds had thinned.

The Haiku regulars were still showing up of course, but with their sad faces on. Along with Sandy's and my frown the bar was not the happy joint it was supposed to be. Ma & Pa did their best to cheer us up. It wasn't quite helping.

I overhead them talking by the stage when they thought I was in the kitchen.

"Ococ and now Tiwaka?" Ma was whispering. "It's too much for him."

I peeked around the koa tree. Pa was nodding and shaking his head slowly at the same time. "What did Wailani say?"

"Nothing, she's not back yet. Without both her and Tiwaka, it's a good thing we're slow. We're pretty shorthanded with both of them gone." Ma paused for several moments and I imagined she might be looking around to see if anyone would hear her next question.

"I've been thinking, maybe we should get him a new puppy and a baby parrot?"

I heard Pa grunt but without seeing his face I couldn't tell if it was an approving grunt or not.

"He's got a brand new baby girl. That's enough baby energy for the moment wouldn't you think?"

"I know, I know," Ma continued, thinking out loud more than anything. "He's got all the family he would ever need. I just hate to see him so sad..."

Pa moved in close and hugged Ma, her tears moving lightly on the breeze blowing my way.

"It's gonna be fine. Somehow," Pa reassured her.

"He's *our* baby you know!" Ma sniffled. "You saw him this morning didn't you?"

"Yes, I did." Pa confirmed, solemnly.

They were both silent for a long moment and I considered making my stealthy exit. Something made me pause though, listening further. I shouldn't have, it pushed me over the edge.

"I loved that silly parrot too, you know," Ma said, breaking down into sobs.

"Me too honey, me too."

~~~

I finally had to make my stealthy exit upon hearing the squeaky brakes of our favorite tour guide, crawling down the gravel driveway slowly. Mark of Maui Guidebook & Guided Tours had a van full and was intent on not over running the tight turn into our parking area, again.

Just missing the coconut tree, that had jumped out in front the last time, he felt compelled with success to ring the large brass ship's bell attached to the roof of the old Dodge Sprinter diesel.

He was a fine driver but that turn had been engineered for mopeds and pedestrians at best. The Kihei Ice guys, pulling in right behind them, never even attempted it, opting to ferry the hundred pound bags on their dollies.

Goldberg, or Mark as some knew him, lived up to his name. When he showed up with a load of tourists it was indeed like an iceberg made of gold had run into our cash register. He always brought the big spenders and this afternoon was no different.

"Aloha!" Mark announced grandiosely, stepping down from his siderunner and opening the sliding door behind him, all in one graceful move.

Stepping out gingerly first was an elderly lady holding Mark's hand on her right and a beautiful ukulele in her left. Her understated, almost royal purple mumu shimmered in the light. Behind her another elegantly decorated woman, not much younger, moved down the steps.

"I brought the band!" Mark announced. He looked at me as I approached and said a bit less loudly, "I heard you guys could use a little," he looked around, "you know. .. cheering up."

I disagreed that we were at that point yet, but I thanked him with a handshake and a pat on the shoulder.

"These guys are good!" Mark announced. "The Joy Strummers of Aledo, Texas," he said catching the offered hand of each elderly lady.

I nodded respectfully to each of them as they moved their elegantly decorated sandals down into the gravel of our parking area.

"They're actually *from Texas*," Mark whispered. "Nice folks. Really."

Each of the ladies held what appeared to be a professional ukulele masterpiece in their hands. Finally the two men in the group exited the van.

Their leader, the youngest among them, had on an antique Aloha shirt tailored perfectly for his impressive frame. Tall and footballish he waved his hands over their heads.

"Ladies and Jim," Pat Kemp announced with a booming twinge of comedy in his voice. "These fine folks at Tiwaka's Tiki Bar & Grill are in need of a good solid gospel classic." Leaning down to the lady with the kukui nuts and gems necklace, he whispered, "What do you think Auntie? One For the Ages?"

She smiled up at the young whippersnapper and nodded, "Yes, in C of course."

As spiritual songs go this one was right up there with the best, perhaps because it was being performed for our direct benefit. And, as our luck would have it they were excellent ukulele strummers.

The oldest lady, with the kukui nut and large sparkling gem necklace was picking her strings like a young pro. I couldn't help but notice she was tapping her right foot, nodding her head with the beat and swinging her hips, all while plucking sweet notes from her polished mahogany uke.

I think they were intending on performing a second song, right there in the parking gravel until a little trade wind rain moved in from the sea cliffs.

"Come on in!" I waved, moving toward the covered bar.

Several of them made for the round bamboo tables. The others filled up the bar stools quickly and I gravitated to my position again as bartender.

Sandy ducked into the kitchen to work up some pupus and Ma & Pa went to the tables taking orders. This was par for the bar, from zero to sixty in two seconds. Suddenly I was busy enough to distract me from Tiwaka, and then just as suddenly it was sixty back to zero.

"Hey, where's the parrot?" The Kihei Ice guy asked, two hundred pound bags on his dolly.

Everyone at the bar turned to look at him, putting their fingers up to their lips. "Shusssh!"

"What?" he asked. "OK, OK," he shrugged. I saw Pa walk over to talk to him on the side.

Mark, the tour driver asked kindly. "Any word at all?"

I shook my head, working real hard to keep my emotions in check. Last thing I wanted to do was tear up in front of a bunch of kind old ladies who would all want to console me at the same time.

"Nada," I finally managed.

"It's like he's on a walkabout," Sandy added, walking in with two trays of our signature plate of coconut fried Mahimahi skewers on a bed of sweetened sprouts. "You know, like they do in Australia, they just take off for a while." She walked behind me and sat down both trays on the bar. Leaning over to me she patted my shoulder and kissed me on the cheek. "They always come back."

Nodding, I turned back to my work, my distraction.

"My wife's a saint you know," I said. "What you drinking today, Mark?" A touch of cheerfulness was finding its way back into my voice.

He grinned and looked to Pat, sitting next to him. "You have GOT to try this," turning back to me he continued. "That Coco Loco Moco smoothie is the bomb!"

"You got it," I turned back to the refrigerator for some of the ingredients.

"I'll have one of those, too," Pat said. "But, put two extra shots of rum in mine!"

Turning back to the bar, I laid out bananas, papaya, star fruit and chunks of fresh coconut.

"That's gonna give you only two shots you know," knowing Mark's recipe for this was different.

Pat turned toward Mark with a confused look.

"I'm driving, dude," Mark shrugged.

"OK, then. Make it three shots!"

Four minutes later I had them both served and moved down the bar. In another ten minutes everyone had a glass, coconut or straw in their hands. It was beginning to feel a little like it used to, smiling faces, colorful concoctions at the bar and even more colorful characters drinking them.

I turned back to the bottles on the wall and saw Tiwaka's empty perch there between the vodka bottles. It was painfully vacant. Looking under the bar, right next to my coconut opening machete I found a glass jar of chocolate covered organic GMO-free cashews I had purchased at Mana Foods a week before.

I picked them up, took one out and ate it of course, and then sat it up on the perch. He would be back for them one day.

"To Tiwaka!" Pat announced to the crowd.

"To Tiwaka!" I raised my voice with the others.

After the toast and everyone returned to their conversations, I snuck another chocolate cashew out of the jar. If he didn't hurry back they would all be gone!

Sandy was taking her time talking to each and every one of the ukulele players. They all seem fascinated with her as well. She was stopped in front of the lady with the amazing kukui nut necklace.

"I must say," Sandy admired. "I've never imagined a kukui necklace could be so dazzling, the jewels really make it...are they diamonds?"

"Oh," the elderly lady demurred. "Only one of them is," gently touching one of the large gems between two kukui nuts. "It is a very special necklace, from my third husband."

Sandy smiled and nodded. "Your third?"

"Oh yes, Tommy. My favorite to be sure."

Sandy looked around trying to guess which guy might be Tommy. The elderly lady noticed and laughed sweetly. She reached out to Sandy's hand and gently added.

"Honey, I've outlived all three of them. God rest their souls."

"Oh," Sandy said, a bit surprised. "Sorry about…"

"Don't be young lady. It's just the way it worked out. Someone's got to outlive somebody."

I moved back to the end of the bar to check on my two Coco Loco Moco smoothie customers. They were both smiling, a good sign for any bartender with a new recipe.

"Well, is it what you thought it would be?" I asked, cleaning mugs with my bamboo fabric towel.

"How many shots of rum did you actually put in mine?" Pat asked.

"Three," I replied with a raised eyebrow. He nodded a little.

"Of course, our shot glasses are a bit oversized," I laughed, holding up half of an empty coconut.

"No way!" Pat exclaimed. His expression wasn't one of disbelief but rather one of amazement.

I got a good laugh out of that. "No worries, just kidding." I slid a plate of coconut fried Mahimahi skewers on a bed of sweetened sprouts to that magic spot of the bar – right in front of a customer.

"I feel like I've either had too much to drink too fast or have fallen in love!" Pat guessed, running his hands through his hair.

"Must be the company," I said with some authority.

Mark looked at both of us and quickly added, "Don't look at me!"

Pat leaned over and put his arm around the tour driver and laughed. "Love ya like a brother, but…" he leaned in a little closer. "You've got to tell me who *that* is?"

Both of them looked behind me, forcing me to turn as well.

"Wailani!" I exclaimed, giving her a big hug and kiss.

"Wow," I heard Pat remark quietly behind me. "Is he married to both of them?"

Mark started laughing, too hard to explain, so I turned around with my arm around the stunning Polynesian beauty with the long black hair, big brown eyes and a secret few men could handle.

"May I introduce to you, Miss Wailani - Maui's most eligible woman!"

Wailani bowed playfully and blew kisses out over the small group behind the stools.

Wild applause followed, and calls for free drinks, naturally.

"I've got news," she whispered into my ear, getting Pat's attention again. He wasn't quite convinced she wasn't my second wife yet. Sandy came up quickly, hugged Wailani too and took my other arm. I had them both now, a beauty in each arm. Pat was aghast and Mark was holding onto the bar, laughing harder than a mynah bird full of fermented berries.

I pulled Sandy into a huddle with Wailani, there behind the bar, in front of everyone and quickly found myself in that deep dark cave of apprehension.

"Did you find anything?" I asked. "You and your friends?"

Sandy hugged me tightly which went well with me holding my breath.

"He's safe," she whispered with some great deal of wonderment in her sweet voice.

"Maururu," Sandy whispered, using Tahitian to give thanks.

I couldn't quite say anything, but my eyes asked for more.

"The Honu saw him nearly fall from the sky several times during the storm. Over the channel. They thought he would surely die."

My breath stopped again.

"He somehow made it to O'ahu," Wailani said, exhaustion in her voice now.

"O'ahu?" I managed to ask incredulously. "O'ahu! That's over a hundred miles from here."

Sandy moved between Wailani and I, whispering to her, hugging her tightly. I felt some measure of almost religious gratitude move between them. Wailani's hands went to Sandy's cheeks wiping tears away lovingly.

"I must rest a while," Wailani said softly.

When I heard that I did notice she looked extremely tired, and thinking about what she may have just endured to get this information it was no surprise.

But, I had one more question. "Where on O'ahu?" I inadvertently said this a little louder, my voice full of excitement. It was then that I noticed a crowd had gathered around the bar in front of us, practically pushing Mark and Pat into the koa wood.

Wailani bowed and retreated into the back, but Sandy turned to the crowd, took my hand and held it up high in victory.

"Tiwaka is in Waikiki!" she shouted with joy.

A great roar erupted and I don't know if anyone could hear me call out for free drinks between my fight with sobs of happiness. It didn't matter; they did hear my first of many toasts a few moments later.

"To Waikiki!"

~~~

It was sometime after his third Coco Loco Moco that Pat told me he and The Joy Strummers of Aledo, Texas were going to Waikiki, on tomorrow's afternoon flight.

"We'll be glad to meet up with Tiwaka for you," he offered through the ground fog of our famous coconut drink.

I had already arranged for Mark to leave his crew of ukulele strummers here at the bar cabins, as they were a bit too celebratory to go back to the hotels. Mark lived close by anyhow and would return at 9 A.M. Yet, that hour seemed too soon for some of these musicians as I looked around. A few were dancing on the tables while others surrounding the table occasionally caught them. Ma & Pa were laughing so hard it was difficult for them to keep the revelers from hurting themselves.

I turned back to Pat, his travel plans working into an idea of my own. We would close the bar for a few days, without Tiwaka it really wasn't much fun anyhow.

"Why don't we *all* go to Waikiki, together?" I asked.

Pat smiled, but immediately turned to the elderly lady with the diamond and kukui nut necklace as she put her arm around him, leaning into his shoulder and smiling at me with a certain joy only decades of happiness could conjure. Her long necklace hung down to the bar.

"We appear to have added to our entourage Emma Jane," Pat said.

Emma Jane fished her diamonds out of Pat's open coconut and smiled up at me. "I feel a song coming on…" Turning she went to gather the Joy Strummers of Adele, Texas.

Pat offered his hand to mine and as I shook it vigorously we both smiled at what looked to be a fine adventure shaping up.

"Waikiki!" he said, a glimmer of playfulness creeping up into his face.

"Waikiki!" I echoed. The very word itself had always flowed so gracefully with my breath whenever I had the opportunity to utter it. After a moment I asked "Are you folks playing any gigs there?"

Pat sat back and laughed a little. "Yes we are! Free concerts on the beach, in the park, the Aquarium, the Shell and anywhere they'll have us."

"Perfect," I said, not sure if I said it out loud or only whispered it to myself.

Sandy came up just then, breathing hard from catching the last of the table dancers on their way down.

"Oh baby," she hugged me. "Tiwaka is safe."

"What do you think about taking Baby Kiawe with us to O'ahu?" I asked her. "On a Tiwaka rescue mission?"

Sandy thought about that for several moments. She then unconsciously looked down to her chest. "Well," she admitted. "I need to take that baby wherever I go, and I have to go now don't I?"

"I'll carry her in the front pack," I volunteered, loving that part almost as much as tucking her in at night. "Maybe she can help us somehow, you know, find Tiwaka."

Sandy snuggled up to me and looked up to smile, a few tears in her eyes.

I kissed her hair and turned, along with Pat, to watch the elderly ladies of the Joy Strummers gather together, bring their ukuleles up and begin playing.

"Perfect," I surely said out loud this time as they began *Over the Rainbow*.

~~~

On Time Airline

In the tropics the first thing a visitor notices is the general lack of respect for time. More precisely I suppose it is a lack of respect for timekeeping. Time here is quite special, but clocks are an aberration. Meeting your friends at the beach, or the mall, or even at Tiwaka's was most successfully arranged by targeting broad terms such as "before dark" or "after I get back from surfing" rather than totally unrealistic concepts such as "6:00".

That cultural aspect of Hawaii has suffered extensively under the recent improvements made at the airports, specifically with Hawaiian Airlines. You simply have to play by rules of efficiency and schedules to catch one of their planes. HAL, as they have always been known became an acronym for "Hawaiian Already Left". That's what you would hear if you got to the gate even one minute late.

You don't get to be number one in on-time performance nationwide by waiting for hung-over ukulele players and their friends from the responsible bar.

"I'm sorry sir," I heard from the agent at the counter. "You appear to have missed your flight. I can put you on standby for the remaining three flights to Honolulu." Before I could complain she added, "But, I'm afraid they are all booked full."

I took a moment before turning back to look at the Joy Strummers, Ma & Pa, Sandy and the porter waiting to tag our large pile of luggage. None of them were in shape for a disappointment.

Turn I did though, keeping my head down to avoid the inevitable mind-reading that eye contact encourages. Sandy, of course, didn't need to see my eyes to read my mind.

"They're full?"

"Oh no!" I heard as a collective groan from the Joy Strummers.

Pat added, "We've got Mai Tais to drink in Waikiki!"

I held my hand up high. It might have appeared that I was asking for a moment of silence. It wasn't anything like that. It was a way I had found worked well over the years when trying to gather another idea from the cosmos. Like an antenna searching for a cell phone signal, my fingers wiggled a little and more times than not I came up with something. I know that sounds a bit far out, and thank God you think so. Nonbelievers - they give me an edge.

"I've got another idea!" I announced, excited that it had actually worked again. "Let me make a quick call." I ignored Pat, who was getting on his cell as well, no doubt making arrangements with another airline. I ignored several of the older ladies sitting down, looking exasperated. I did wink at Sandy and smile. My phone call answered on the second ring and I looked away from those intoxicating eyes so I could communicate with mere mortals.

"Air Maui, may I help you?"

"Yes, hi. Is Steve there? Eggers?"

"Sure, may I ask who is calling please?"

"Yes, it's the crew from Tiwaka's Tiki Bar & Grill."

There was a moment of silence before the nice young girl on the other end processed what she had heard.

"Tiwaka who?" she asked.

I got this a lot, especially when talking to anyone outside the confines of the east Maui jungles. I would have to send her a brochure.

"Tiwaka Tiki, he'll know."

"Please hold," she politely said, escaping into the nice background Hawaiian music. I looked up and saw Pat talking on his phone, no doubt trying to arrange a ride as well. The race was on!

"Hey, what the heck is a parrot doing on the phone?" Eggers asked jokingly, coming onto the line.

"Yo bro!" I said loud enough to get Pat's attention. "The gang's all here, at the airport ... stuck."

"No kidding," Eggers laughed. "Why's that? Miss the Hawaiian Air flight?" I could hear him laughing in the background.

"Yeah, you know how it is," I acknowledged. "I just got a feeling to call you, you know. I've got thirty people that need to make it to O'ahu this afternoon...."

"Thirty?" Eggers exclaimed. "Did you really say thirty?"

My heart sank a little at the reality of my request.

"Well, yes," I said a little meekly. "And their luggage."

The line was silent for several moments.

"Steve?" I said softly.

"Hold on...."

The line was silent a full minute. All I could hear were a few voices in the room on his side discussing something. At least it wasn't an immediate "you're fricking crazy" or "I'm sorry but what planet did you say you were from?"

Just then Pat held up his hands in victory.

"We're First Class on the first flight in the morning!"

I saw a few smiles rise up with that, but we still had the rest of today to kill. I raised my index finger up to signal I had something still in the works. At least I hoped I did.

"Did you really say thirty plus luggage?" Eggers was back on the line, asking me to repeat again my ridiculous request.

"Look, I know weight is an issue. Some of these ladies only weigh ninety pounds and that's with their jewelry on."

"Yeah, yeah. How soon can you get over here?"

My grin delayed my answer for a full three or four micro seconds. "Ten minutes?"

"Make it nine, we gotta land before dark you know!" Eggers was yelling, but in a nice happy sort of way.

"Really?" I had to say it.

"Yeah, yeah. I was going to ferry five birds over anyhow for maintenance. I'll throw in the sixth one for some Coco Loco Mocos next time I drop into Tiwaka's."

"Wow, look," I offered. "I'll cover the fuel. We were going to give it up to the airline anyway."

"Deal," Eggers said. "But, look, seriously. You gotta have everyone here, and their luggage, in ten minutes or it's a no go. Got it?"

"On my way!" I almost hung up. "Thanks Steve!"

"Yeah, yeah," he said. "Nine minutes now, we're fueling..."

I hung up and announced to everyone.

"We've got a ride!"

Everyone looked over at me and my silly grin. "But, we've got to get to the east ramp in nine minutes."

"What?" I think most everyone said that in unison.

Running up to the porter, giving him a fresh hundred and our need for a bus, I turned to Pat.

"Cancel that first class ride dude. We're going super duper class!"

"OK," he laughed. "Where the heck is the east ramp anyhow?"

"You'll see."

Sandy came up to me and whispered as we boarded the suddenly appearing shuttle. "Air Maui?"

"Yeah, this is gonna be a blast!" I hugged her a little. "Don't tell them yet, OK?"

"No way, it's *your* surprise."

"Yep", I said as we rounded the back road to the opposite side of the airport, luggage, ukuleles and a group of old ladies who couldn't let an opportunity to sing get by them. They were into another spiritual hymn, humming and singing and rocking with the bus.

"My all time favorite flying machine," I whispered to Sandy, kissing her for probably the hundredth time today.

Three minutes later we were pulling up into the Air Maui parking lot. I watched everyone's faces closely, but most of them were still looking

88

for an airplane parked somewhere. A few of the ladies were pointing far down the ramp at the private jets lined up.

"Is that Oprah's?" someone asked.

Another answered no, hers would be bigger.

Eggers walked out from his small office, all grins and arms.

"Welcome to Air Maui, everyone!"

I could see him counting heads and nodding with some satisfaction that many of my crew were indeed only ninety pounds. Two big guys ran out after him and were directed to our luggage.

"OK everyone," Eggers said in a loud booming - pay attention for safety - voice. "Stay away from the rear rotors. The lovely ladies in aloha shirts will guide you to your seats."

Pat looked at me and laughed out loud. "Helicopters?"

"Finest kine!" I added, handing my Tiwaka's credit card to Eggers.

"Run it for whatever you need. Can you accept airline tickets for some of it?"

Eggers nodded. "I can, but only because they love me."

Four minutes later we were all boarded on six A-Star Eurocopters, music headphones on and watching in true fascination as our airships rose smoothly straight up into the clear Maui air.

As we crossed the coastline at Ma'alaea and flew directly between the islands of Maui, Lanai and Molokai I found myself entranced once again. The sea was rolling with the trade winds in the same direction we were flying, a following sea always brought good luck. The green mysteries of Molokai passed to my right as whales luxuriated just below.

Sandy had her forehead against the window. Baby Kiawe was tucked securely into her lap, napping the entire time, every bit the angel.

Beauty is such a distraction. It was a wonder I could ever get anything done. Thankfully, my job never asked me to ignore the obvious. In fact, when I considered what we really did at the bar, at the bay and in the tree house, beauty was the one driving force that made it all real, that gave everything that hue of importance. Perhaps it was beauty that distracts us from ignorance.

I took a couple of deep relaxing breaths, watching the sea rush below me. It was easy to let the view take me away again, to my happy place. Yet, here I was an hour away from having to search for my best buddy somewhere in Waikiki. My lost friend, alone and confused in a strange city, needed rescue. The air cavalry was on its way.

~~~

Suzi "Mojo" Coleman

"Mojo baby....mojo baby..."

"Oh you poor thing," Suzi whispered to the delusional bird, repeating himself constantly. She sat at a booth across from the bar area of La Mariana stroking the purple and yellow feathers of her newest patient. He was so cute; he matched her Aloha shirt perfectly.

"I came in last night to clean, after the bar closed, and found him curled up on the shelf, surrounded by the vodka bottles," Rasha said softly as she leaned over and touched the trembling parrot's head for just a moment. "Well, I've got to punch out, thanks for getting here so early Suzi."

"Mahalo for calling Rasha, this one looks to be in pretty rough shape."

"The cook will be here around 10:00 if you need anything else," Rasha said on her way out, her long aloha print mumu having replaced her gray cleaning jumpsuit.

Suzi looked back down to the parrot lying in her lap. He was breathing slowly and occasionally opened his right eye to see if she were still there.

"I'll get you back in shape, don't you worry little guy." Suzi reached into her oversized bag and fished out a special red scarf to wrap around the parrot.

"How did your feathers get so beaten up? Has someone been hurting you?"

"...mojo baby...mojo..." Tiwaka continued to chant with as much breath as he could muster.

"Mojo?" Suzi repeated. "Is that the name of the cat you got in a fight with?" She stood up slowly, cradling the bird and walked over to the bar.

"You no doubt need some water, and maybe a snack."

Suzi went behind the bar, found a small bowl and a bag of cashews. A cheap digital camera was tucked beside a stack of plastic ash trays.

"Here you go," Suzi announced, pouring water into the bowel and laying out several cashews alongside. "Drink up, and I mean that in the healthiest of ways, even if we are in a bar."

She watched as Tiwaka found enough strength to stand and drink. Meanwhile her curiosity could hold out no further with the camera.

Flipping the camera around several times until she found the power switch she then searched for the scroll button. It was just about then that Tiwaka burped, loud and proud.

"Wow, feeling better are you?"

"Mo...Jo!" Tiwaka said, happy to getting back into some kind of a groove. He went for his second cashew when his head started spinning again. As he stumbled, Suzi dropped the camera on the bar and caught the bag of bones as he collapsed.

"Well, I'd say you look a bit like a rock and roller who's been on the road a week too long." She carried the parrot outside to the palm tree shaded hammock, wrapped him lightly in her special red scarf again and lay him down gently. "Take a nap; I'll be over here in this comfy chair."

Suzi sat on the deck a few feet away from the hammock and took another look at the digital camera. She scrolled through the images thinking she must have missed quite a wild costume party. Everyone was dressed up as famous and young tiki personalities. Even the bartender....Joe Bar...looked to be in his twenties.

"How did he do that?" she whispered to herself.

She kept moving through the images, amazed to see such great costumes.

"Oh my god...is that Gardner McKay?" She kept moving through the images. "Don Ho? No way...with Don the Beachcomber?"

She held the camera out again to look at it, spinning it slowly through her hands looking for the hint of the trick that someone must be playing with her. These people weren't wearing costumes! How could a modern digital camera, she wondered, have images of young famous tiki guys who had died years ago? Maybe it had been used to take pictures of old photographs? She felt better with that explanation.

Eventually, she got to the pictures that had Tiwaka in them and that's when she felt the first of several chills move along her neck. She zoomed in on the first one thinking perhaps it had to be a different parrot. The close up confirmed it was her patient, tattered feathers and all.

She looked over at the sleeping parrot swinging lightly in the breeze. "Oh my god, if only you could talk!"

~~~

Tiwaka had his first dream that afternoon, in the hammock of the La Mariana Sailing Club. It started off softly, like any good dream will, with a light breeze of sound something akin to music. He was walking amongst tall trees, climbing a hill whose open summit he could easily see approaching. Soon, he was there by himself, watching fanciful clouds sweep between him and the blue space above. His feathers moved in the breeze, still tattered and torn in places.

Scanning the distant horizon in all directions he saw no other islands, only the one he stood atop. Just as he began to get an overwhelming feeling of loneliness a shape appeared in the sky, coming his way. He watched it approach until he could see that it too was some manner of bird creature. It had large wings, much larger than his. It glided then pumped, glided and then pumped again, propelling this …. man? Yes, it was a man with wings and he was flaring now to land next to him.

Tiwaka took a few steps back as the man stumbled once and then got his footing again. His wings immediately folded back behind him and he stood tall and confident, smiling.

"What kind of bird are you?" Tiwaka said, or thought, or dreamed. He wasn't quite sure how he was talking so easily.

"Ah, my friend. I'm no bird, no more than you are."

Tiwaka didn't understand what that meant, but in this dream there was no confusion. There was only fascination.

He walked over slowly to Tiwaka and picked a place on the ground next to him where he gently sat himself down. "I'm no man either, you see." He moved a little to get more comfortable. "We're both quite a bit more." He had to adjust his tall frame one more time. "We're here now, you and I, as ambassadors." The man with wings turned away and looked out over the horizon, as if he might see something there. After a moment he didn't and looked back to the ground.

"I used to be a pilot you know. I used to be young..."

It was then that Tiwaka noticed the man was quite old, perhaps as much as ninety. How he could manage flying suddenly became a mystery.

"I used to climb inside fighter planes, jets, and go places I never thought I could ever get to. But I did." He looked over at Tiwaka, his sharp blue eyes un-dulled by time or age.

Tiwaka tried to ask a question but it eluded him, lost in some new flurry of thoughts and images.

"I know how it is at first, believe me. Lightning is a bitch, ain't it?" the winged man said. "You'll find yourself more and more comfortable with your new powers soon." He turned back to look out at the horizon. He blinked several times and for a moment turned his face away, bringing his hand up to his eyes, wiping them softly.

"What do you mean, I'm not a bird, and you're not a man?" Tiwaka asked, unsure of how he had vocalized it.

The winged man turned back to Tiwaka and smiled. "I suppose it's a bit of a perfect analogy, really. You see, we've all got wings ... just some of us don't know why." He turned back to watch the horizon. Tiwaka noticed the winged man's shoulders sag a little.

He didn't speak for a few moments and Tiwaka wondered if he was done. The horizon did seem to hold some fascination that Tiwaka now enjoyed as well. It was undulating softly under the brilliant light from the sky, as if a billion billion beings were dancing there. "You see all those, out there on the horizon?" The winged man continued. "They can soar, but some don't know how." He placed his hand gently on Tiwaka's shoulder. "I know how, and now you do too Tiwaka." The wind moved suddenly between them, fluttering the man's large wings as well as Tiwaka's.

"I'm here to help you, and I hope that you will do the same with those you meet." He looked intently at Tiwaka with his piercing blue eyes, a glint of pleading sparkling in those pools of light. "You know ... to help them fly."

An overwhelming happiness suddenly invaded Tiwaka's mind, as if he might have discovered how to make his own chocolate, but better. The winged man's supplication had released something inside Tiwaka that brought all the flurry of images and thoughts into a crystalline focus. It was like knowing all the ingredients that went inside the chocolate too.

Tiwaka looked at the man again, as he now stood up, suddenly appearing young and strong again. His wings spread out to block the light from behind him. Looking down at Tiwaka, his grin was infectious. His feathers appeared to be fluttering under a great effortless tension.

"Tiwaka, we're all proud of you. Not every middle aged creature finds their magic like you have." He leaned over to touch him on the top of his feathered head. "You've got your mojo back now, don't you?"

~~~

Suzi had sat all morning and most of the afternoon with the injured parrot. When he finally stirred, hours after she had placed him in the hammock she quickly went over to the shade of the palms.

"Well, how are you feeling now, little one?" She gently unwrapped her special red scarf from around the bird, smiling. "I bet you were dreaming weren't you?" She smoothed out his ruffled feathers and ran her finger lightly down his leg to his talons. "You must be quite the special bird." Turning to see if anyone was close by and seeing no one was she whispered. "I saw the pictures. Quite the crowd you were hanging with, yes?"

Tiwaka sat up as best he could and looked at his nurse. He bobbed his head lightly. The dream was still fresh in his mind and it was taking a little longer to transition back to the world. He looked up at the smiling beauty with her red scarf. Something came to him, a name perhaps, a greeting. He wasn't sure but felt compelled to say it.

"Kukana."

Suzi sat back, surprised. Kukana was her Hawaiian name, something she hadn't used in years. She paused for a long moment, watching the bird closely. Whatever was going on: this bird showing up at La Mariana, the pictures of it and the long dead tiki personalities and now knowing her secret Hawaiian name, it was enough to cause her some consternation.

"Yes. Kukana, indeed. What is your name?"

Tiwaka looked at her first with his left eye and then after a moment turned to see her with his right. It painted a nice picture.

"Tiwaka. Tiwaka."

Suzi smiled. "Very good, Tiwaka Tiwaka. Let me go get you some more water. I'll be back in a few minutes." She stood up to go back into the bar, still holding the camera in her hand.

~~~

"Yo! Tiwaka!"

Tiwaka was feeling quite a bit better after sleeping most of the day but hearing voices calling his name made him think he might still be a bit groggy.

"Hey, shipmate, let's sail!"

Tiwaka looked around, through the stand of coconut trees and out to the shimmering water where several sailboats decorated the small dock. Someone was waving vigorously with his arm.

"Over here! Tiwaka!"

Tiwaka rotated his shoulders and flexed his wings. Both spoke back but felt significantly better than the day before. Quickly he hopped down to the ground. Suzi was nowhere to be seen, or anyone else, just the guy on the dock waving an arm and shouting his name.

"I need your help on the bow, spotting turtles!" The man spoke loudly now but had quit shouting.

Just behind him was a familiar looking boat ... the schooner he had landed on after the storm! Immediately, Tiwaka tried to fly over to him. He got a couple of feet off the ground and felt his muscles tighten up again. Landing hard he fell over to one side but got up quickly, a little embarrassed.

Suddenly, the *Tiki* captain was standing next to him. Tiwaka looked up at him in surprise, but managed to bob his head hello.

"Need a lift, my friend?"

Tiwaka shook his head no and started walking toward the dock. Looking up to his friend he found a smile matching his own.

"It's a beautiful afternoon for a sail, Tiwaka."

Tiwaka knew it was as well, it was a beautiful day for everything.

~~~

Waikiki Beach

Our helicopters were rapidly approaching O'ahu's southern crescent, where Diamond Head was holding back a marching army of tall buildings from proceeding further east. We were low over the water, perhaps only two hundred feet and slowly turning toward the west and the airport. There the lava fields of white concrete were not quite so high, but still extended down to the coastline.

Just behind, the green jungled mountains of the Ko'olau range stood proud and happy that they were still more impressive than what man had wrought below. Rainbows winked from each valley as we moved along the shore, hinting of magic to be found deep inside.

Sandy was oohing and aahing, even above the noise of our flying machine. It was an impressive site, this gathering place of both people and the aina, the land. Some might argue it had been overdeveloped, with a great deal of evidence at hand. Others could easily point out a certain embracing of similar goals by man, reaching to the heavens with their buildings just as the mountains did only a few miles away. I suppose if man had the same amount of time to fashion their expression, like the millions of years that nature had, ours might be similarly beautiful.

I had only a moment to think on this before my mind was invaded by thoughts of finding Tiwaka, down there, in the midst of all that … humanity. The density appeared overwhelming. How could one find a lost anything down there?

One advantage I did see right away, though, was that Tiwaka's colorful feathers would stand out among all the textures, colors and shadows that I was seeing.

"We'll be landing in two minutes," our pilot said. We were in the lead and headed toward the southern end of the massive Honolulu International Airport. One of the runways there was practically an island in itself, connected only by a taxiway to the large complex. We swooped into an area just to the right of that, where I saw dozens of small commuter planes, and other helicopters. The large 747s and Airbus' were all parked a mile away at the main terminal, across another couple of runways.

The pilot rotated our helicopter around so that as we touched down we could see the other five helicopters approaching from the sea. I flashed on an old war movie I had seen once, *Apocalypse Now* I believe. There was a scene similar to this with a large group of helicopters approaching a tropical beach scene. I just hoped we would have a better ending, a much better one.

~~~

The good ship *Tiki* cleared the channel just east of the Reef Runway, with Tiwaka standing watch on the bow, very slowly flapping his fully extended wings. The boat was moving so slowly through the light chop it appeared to Gardner McKay that the bird was pulling them through the water with wing power alone.

Tiwaka was well aware these same exercises back on Maui had given rise to his first flights, and with any luck they would again. He looked up for a moment, away from the water and up into the air. He would be back up there soon. For a brief moment he had a little panic thinking about how he was supposed to get back to Maui. He sure couldn't fly that far and that ride on the thunder was a one way trip.

"See any turtles, Tiwaka?" Gardner McKay shouted from the helm at the stern. The open ocean was just beginning to rock them slightly.

Tiwaka folded back his right wing, keeping his left one extended to point. "Port bow, Captain. Clear!" Tiwaka was amazed at how well he could communicate now. He remembered the short conversation with the winged man from his dream and now with Gardner. It was if some people, perhaps those that knew why they had wings, could understand him better. In any case it was exhilarating. It was no longer a struggle to work words up from deep inside his belly, beating his wings and stomping his feet to simply say "Aloha."

The sea turtles were just to his left, keeping up with their slow pace through the small waves, occasionally looking up at him and waving a flipper. Tiwaka was too busy concentrating on his wing exercises to do much more than nod to them.

The sea just ahead was shimmering in the low light of an approaching sunset. This made it impossible to see deeply into the water, but it also made the turtles glimmer when they broke the surface to breathe.

He could feel his muscles responding to the workout; He felt them lose some of their tightness, felt the power sneak back slowly into his wings. His feathers were still a bit of a mess and would remain so for some weeks until new ones could grow in.

He was especially distraught about his missing tail feathers. The last of the damaged ones had fallen out only a few moments ago, leaving him looking more and more like, in his mind, a penguin. With any luck, he thought, his wings would be ready to fly when his tail feathers grew back. He would need both to stay airborne.

Captain McKay was missing his pipe. It wasn't that it was lost, but rather that it no longer existed. He had become rather fond of the sweetened tobacco in a mesquite bowl gently nestled between his teeth. It was simply not available anymore. Some things, he knew now, were relics of an increasingly distant past.

The helm felt good in his hands, and for that he was quite thankful. His schooner was as responsive as she had always been and just as beautiful, the water kissing her hull in reverence. The clear and pristine weather off of Waikiki was the stuff of dreams, and, indeed he felt he was living through a very realistic one. There was nothing to complain about, only small mysteries of detail.

He still had his friends at La Mariana Sailing Club and on occasion he met a new one, although that was becoming less and less common. Tiwaka was a gem, and he hoped the bird would stick around for a while.

Something wasn't quite right though. The air moved through his hair but then other times it felt to him as if *he* were the very air itself. Other sailboats never gave way to *Tiki*, as if they couldn't even see him. And, most confusing, as he often sailed past the small cinder cone in Honolulu called Punchbowl he felt a powerful surge of near crippling weakness. His heart almost fled his chest with a pull toward a particular high rise building nestled at the bottom of its slope. Something about it called to him.

He found the green hill surrounded by concrete quite easily again and stared at it, feeling the tug increase. He found it exceedingly difficult to concentrate on his sailing, as the helm slid through his fingers.

Tiwaka felt the turn in the boat and looked back to his Captain. He was staring at the mountains with a longing Tiwaka had seen only on a few occasions in his time at the bar. He recognized it immediately, and smiled.

"Ay, Captain," he said to Gardner. "We are off course?"

"Oh Tiwaka, my heart! It is pulling so strongly toward ... there." He pointed toward Punchbowl.

Tiwaka looked himself and saw a sparkle of light, something unusual for a cityscape, moving up slowly from above a high rise there, climbing steadily into blue sky just above the cloud kissed mountains.

"Do you see the star?" Gardner asked, still staring. "Do you see it rising?"

Tiwaka looked back to the stern and smiled. He had indeed. "You, sir, are in love!"

"Aye, Tiwaka, I must be. For I feel my entire being drawn there."

The *Tiki* was now headed directly toward the coastline, as if it might climb the shoreline and ride an invisible wind, above the buildings, toward the rising brilliance of that star, taking Gardner to his love.

"She must be someone quite special my Captain," Tiwaka said. "Someone who still loves you ..."

"Yes ..." Gardner said softly. "The star, Tiwaka! It's still rising!"

Tiwaka watched as it did, and knew intuitively that it would continue to do so. He watched the bow turn again to the east as Gardner corrected to keep from hitting the rocks ahead. His gaze never left the star though.

Tiwaka watched the star growing slowly into a more brilliant display of light and to his surprise he could feel its warmth, its depth of compassion. It must belong to a great artist.

"Who is it, Captain?" Tiwaka finally asked.

Gardner paused for several moments, obviously overcome with emotion. He stood as tall and proud as he could and blew an invisible kiss skyward, toward the star, now growing even larger.

"My sweet, sweet Madeleine."

~~~

Pat had somehow already arranged transport before we even landed. I needed a cell phone signal that good too! By the time the last of the six Air Maui birds had landed there was a big Polynesian Hospitality bus pulling into the parking lot.

It was about an hour prior to sunset before we were rolling toward Waikiki. Baby Kiawe was up and hungry. Sandy and she took a seat in the back. I was walking up and down the long aisle, looking through all the windows.

The ride in was a bit disconcerting along some road they called Nimitz highway. It reminded me of a bad B-movie from the 1960s about time warped Twilight Zone passengers stuck in an industrial district. Warehouses, mattress wholesalers and ugliness finally gave way to Ala Moana and a glimpse of the beautiful sea. The sea, ultimately, had saved Honolulu from itself.

The tour boats next to the Fisherman's Wharf restaurant were busy enticing tourists out for a few drinks and a fabulous sunset. Our large bus rolled past as if we were on a better mission, a mission of discovery. We were headed to Waikiki Beach!

The Joy Strummers were busy singing and laughing and having a grand time. Sandy was smiling from ear to ear and I did at times too. But, I was worried. This was a big city, over a million people. Honolulu was idyllic, beautiful and exciting, but it was also a place where the small things in life could get trampled if not protected. Tiwaka was one of those small things. What was a Maui jungle bird going to do in a big city but get taken advantage of, or worse?

One thing I noticed though, the one thing that surprised me about Honolulu, was how clean it appeared. There were no piles of garbage like you would see in big East Coast cities. The sidewalks were clear, no abandoned cars were evident and the buildings simply glimmered in the orange light of the setting sun.

That made me feel quite a bit better. Tiwaka might get taken advantage of because of his naivety, but at least I felt he wouldn't be gobbled up for someone's dinner.

~~~

Tiwaka was still standing guard on the bow, spotting turtles about every twenty minutes, sometimes dozens of them. Gardner McKay was steering the good ship *Tiki* closer and closer to the beach at Waikiki but appeared to be aiming for a harbor entrance just before the great sandy expanse fronting the grand hotels.

"We'll put in at the Ala Wai for a moment if you don't mind Tiwaka. I've got a tab running at the Chart House there. Tradition and all you know."

"Aye aye Captain," Tiwaka acknowledged. It was all good as far as he was concerned. His strength was returning by the minute and he was feeling much, much better than a day ago. The scenery was magnificent in any direction he looked. He was alive and well and despite looking like a colorful penguin he couldn't complain.

Gardner seemed to be able to maneuver the *Tiki* with the assistance of only the wind. Even in tight spots, like a right turn into the Ala Wai Yacht Harbor, he only required a breath of wind, perhaps that which he could conjure up all by himself. The *Tiki* was not a small boat by any means, yet he handled it like it fit inside one hand.

"Tiwaka, grab that bow line will you buddy?"

"Aye, aye," Tiwaka grabbed it in his beak and jumped down to the dock as smoothly as any seasoned deck hand.

"Tie it off!" Gardner commanded.

"Secure!" Tiwaka answered after wrapping it several times around the cleat.

Gardner made a few more ropes secure and met Tiwaka on the dock, tightening up what the parrot had managed to get done. "Good job buddy. Will you wait here until I see if anyone is at the bar? This place," he said with some concern "can be a bit wild at times."

"Aye, aye," Tiwaka said all the while trying to remember when he started speaking this way. He watched Gardner move down the dock and disappear around a corner. Taking a well deserved deep breath he looked at all the sailboats, feeling like he could enjoy the life of an able bodied sailor. Being able to communicate so easily was still exciting him. Could it have been the lightning? Or something else, he shrugged, rotating his still sore shoulders.

"Whatever," Tiwaka said out loud to himself. "I like it!"

Rapidly approaching footsteps from somewhere caught his attention.

"What is it that you like?" A voice from behind him on the dock asked with just a hint of demand in it.

Tiwaka turned quickly to spot a grizzled old boat type with rag tag clothes and bare feet coming up quickly. His weathered hands were already out for the grab.

"Captain!" Tiwaka squawked as loud as he could. Quickly he tried to fly but only succeeded in falling a couple of feet away. His pursuer stumbled as well, falling a foot away.

"Captain, Captain!" Tiwaka said, already out of breath.

"I got ya ..."

"No, you don't ..." Tiwaka tried to stand up for another launch.

"Yeah I do ..."

Tiwaka felt an incredibly strong hand grab his leg, squeezing so tight he winched in pain. He turned quickly to attempt to bite the ugly, sunburned fingers.

"No you don't you little ..."

Tiwaka never saw the other hand coming. He only remembered being an inch away from taking a chunk of flesh out of his captor. After that thought there was one brief instant where he felt a hard blow to his head, then it all stopped.

"Ha!" the old boat guy said, standing up, a bit bloodied. One hand held the bird's head and the other both legs, in case those talons got busy. "I'll get a few bucks for you now won't I?"

He quickly looked around to check for witnesses and seeing none quickly made his way to Hobron Lane with his prize. Ironically enough he didn't draw much unwanted attention when he merged into the crowds at the corner with Ala Moana Boulevard.

"Hey honey," a tourist remarked to his girlfriend. "Check out the pirate and his parrot."

She squeezed her boyfriend's arm and wrinkled her nose a little at the details her boyfriend seemed to be missing. "Looks like they've both been at sea a little too long."

~~~

Uncle, well someone's uncle no doubt, had given up giving us a sightseeing tour and had joined the Joy Strummers in song. He could steer the large bus just as easily through traffic, pedicabs and jay walkers singing or talking. His voice made you wonder why he was a driver and not hitting the club circuit.

When I asked him about this, as a compliment, he laughed.

"Yeah bruddha, I sing at night at the Halekulani Tuesdays and Thursdays. A quartet." He rounded an especially tight corner where the extra foot or so of clearance he usually had had been gobbled up by a stalled moped. "Come by sometime, I'm the handsome one!"

Sandy pulled on my arm as I stood next to Uncle, pointing out the window.

"I've seen a few people with parrots on their shoulders, getting pictures with tourists." She looked up at me from her seat.

In a block we saw two vendors with Tiwaka-type macaws, sometimes three or four, sitting on their arm or a post, posing for tourists. It seemed a bit absurd to Sandy and me, but it must have been popular. Tourism, good or bad, overdone or perfectly executed always entertained the locals, if only for the fashion statements. I poked Sandy in the shoulder as we both noted the Aloha shirts being worn next to the birds were brighter than their feathers.

As we turned right onto Kalakaua avenue I searched the throngs of people walking hand in hand, laughing or taking pictures. The trees had thousands of birds and the sky dozens, but nowhere did I see Tiwaka.

~~~

Suzi had returned with a nice bowl of water with just a drop of lime juice and found the hammock empty. Looking around quickly she spotted nothing and no one. Hesitantly she looked on the ground for feathers, fearing the worse. There were the gray leftovers from slow moving pigeons and immature coconut buds that the rats had knocked off the palms. But, no Tiwaka.

~~~

Gardner McKay made his way back to the *Tiki* to find his shipmate gone. He too looked up and down the dock for feathers, remembering there must be a dozen cats in residence among the semi-permanently parked sailboats.

"Tiwaka? Buddy?"

He looked up at the masts hoping to see him atop any of the hundred or so crows' nests. Nothing fluttered there but small flags and wind turbines.

Back on board the *Tiki* he searched everywhere, even the liquor cabinet. No Tiwaka.

~~~

The Parrot Master

"I'm no pirate!"

Tiwaka twisted in the hands of his captor but only felt the old boat man's hands squeeze harder.

"Yes. Yes you are a pirate. You shanghaied me back at the dock. Perfect definition I would say!" Tiwaka was still marveling at his command of language, even in such a tight situation.

"Keep talking, bird. You're gonna make me even more money!"

He began a slow jog now, making way through the slow moving shoppers and the surfed-out surfers. Sometimes he stepped into the busy road to clear a mass of people blocking the sidewalk. Each time, someone yelled at him to get out of the road.

"Yeah, yeah!" the pirate grumbled.

"Who would buy an old bird like me?" Tiwaka negotiated. "I don't even have any tail feathers!"

The pirate stopped jogging, ducked into a small alley next to the Kobe Japanese Steak House and turned Tiwaka upside down to look.

"Holy ... what boat did you sink?" The pirate took a moment to spit on the ground, still turning Tiwaka this way and that. "You look like a frickin' penguin!" He started laughing uproariously, ignoring the insulted bird's squawks. "I'll make even more money with a talking penguin!"

He looked out of the alley, left and then right. Liking what he saw he started jogging again on the sidewalk, in the gutter and sometimes in the road. His breathing was becoming labored and Tiwaka figured he might stumble any minute and take them both under any of the dozen large tour buses rolling heavily by.

"Look, I'm sure you can get quite a bit of gold from the likes of me," Tiwaka tried. "But, if you call my boss, he will give you a better ransom."

The pirate looked down at Tiwaka with some interest, but kept jogging, heading east. "Can your boss get me paid tonight?"

Tiwaka felt his head feathers brush by a light pole as his captor stumbled on the sidewalk. He was afraid this guy would hurt him inadvertently any moment.

"No, it would take a couple of days but it would ..."

"I need beer money, bird. Pretty soon I might add." The pirate made the right turn onto Kalia road, turned into the Hilton Hawaiian Village driveway and a few seconds later stopped around the corner from the Benihana's.

Tiwaka wished for the best in the shadows of the building, hoping for a chance at escape as soon as the pirate dropped his guard, and at least one of his hands. He also flashed on how he had been talking with him ... just as easily as the winged man in his dream and Gardner. How could this scoundrel, this birdnapper be someone who ... who knew why he had wings?

The pirate held him tightly though even as he coughed and hacked for a full minute. As a large group of boisterous teenagers milled past the pirate held Tiwaka up to his chest and under his tattered shirt.

Several of the boys looked at them and sneered. One of them came over toward them, but was pulled back by two of the girls.

Tiwaka could hear the pirate's heart racing, perhaps sputtering as well, and the wheezing of his lungs. He could smell weeks' worth of sweat and grime and sadness on his skin as well.

"You should go see a doctor, they have free clinics here, don't they?" Tiwaka asked softly.

The pirate looked at him funny, with a frowning scowl. "Yeah, I'm gonna. Gonna see Doctor Jack Daniels or maybe his assistant, Jim Beam." He laughed a little at his own joke. "Why, what's it to you?"

Some of Tiwaka's anger at his captor was fading into pity. This guy was a 'down on his luck', self destructive hobo who had happened across what he thought was a meal-ticket, or in this case more accurately a drink-ticket.

"It's just ..." Tiwaka began, measuring his words carefully. "... it's just that I seem to only be able to talk to special ..."

"Yo!" the pirate suddenly announced, waving his hand at someone.

Tiwaka quickly spun his head as best he could to see who it was.

"Over here, I got ya a good one tonight, have a looksee, this one ..."

"OK already, quiet down!" An older man walked confidently over to them, a suitcase rolling behind him. He was dressed like a circus barker who might be on his way to the airport. Tiwaka immediately got a bad feeling.

"This here is a talking parrot, no joshing, a regular chatterbox..."

114

"Where did you find him?" the man interrupted.

The pirate held Tiwaka out facing the man for him to inspect. "Wandering all alone down by the Ala Wai boats. Seen him by himself there, lost, for over an hour."

The man looked at Tiwaka, touched his feathers, gently squeezed his legs. "Turn it around, I need to see all of it."

As the pirate turned Tiwaka around, the frightened bird looked at his captor and spoke quietly. "You're special, why are you living like this?"

"Where the heck are his tail feathers?" The man demanded.

"Oh, this one is *special*," the pirate emphasized while looking directly at Tiwaka. "My guess he's off one of those party cruise boats doing double duty as a penguin..."

The man held his hand up for silence. He shook his head slowly as if he didn't want another molecule of conversation. Reaching down he unzipped the main compartment on his carry-on sized bag.

"Twenty bucks," the man said.

The pirate pulled Tiwaka back a bit. "What? No way! He's way too ..."

"Eighteen," the man countered.

Tiwaka was about to complain as well. Were they really talking that small amount of money?

"Come on, a man's gotta live, you know..."

"Sixteen," the man said firmly. The cruelty was thick in his voice.

"OK, already," the pirate conceded. "Geez, sixteen, then."

"Good move, put the bird in my suitcase," the man said pulling out a twenty dollar bill out of his shirt pocket. "I've got to go make some change." He walked over to a shave ice cart.

Tiwaka looked up at the pirate as he was being pushed inside of the suitcase. "Look, I can talk to you because for some reason you are special ..."

"Yeah, oh I'm special all right..."

"Who is this guy?" Tiwaka squeaked in fear. "What will he do with me?"

The man walked back with a rainbow colored shave ice in his hand, and sixteen one dollar bills. He handed them down to the pirate still trying to work the old zipper on the suitcase.

"Hurry up with that will you?" the man said, irritated. His eyes never left several young women walking by in the latest short shorts.

The pirate took the money, kissed the bills knowing he had his alcohol fix made for the evening. The zipper finally moved and as he stuffed Tiwaka into the darkness, he whispered to him.

"Yeah, I'm in a special place all right," zipping the final inch closed. "Hell."

~~~

The Parrot Master enjoyed his shave ice especially well knowing it had been paid for with four dollars that hobo would have wasted on malt liquor. He walked casually along the winding sidewalks of Ft. Derussy, enjoying the wide open spaces the military had preserved from civilian development.

The few minutes before sunset were his favorite. The crowds had gravitated to the beaches and bars, restaurants and hotel balconies. In a couple of hours they would be ready for something else exotic to do, perhaps a nice twenty eight dollar portrait with an authentic Hawaiian parrot. He had been in Honolulu practically his entire life and knew parrots or macaws were not native birds. It didn't matter to the tourists and it didn't matter to him. It was all an illusion anyhow, this paradise gig.

His suitcase rocked back and forth a few times and his newest acquisition was squawking. A swift kick solved that problem.

The bird business had been very good to him. A syndicate of dozens of young aimless winter refugees desperate to make a few bucks and have a bit of fun doing it provided his labor. They made eight dollars for each shoot and he made a cool twenty. All he had to do was keep the parrots in good supply. Between buying up the big birds of recently deceased owners or stealing those that came wandering in on sailboats he kept busy most afternoons. He wasn't getting rich but he was living his dream, albeit the "lite" version. It beat driving trucks in Montana or fishing for shrimp in Louisiana. Actually this job was pretty easy. All he had to do was keep the thieving kids from robbing him blind and round up the birds before midnight.

He crossed Kalia over to Beachwalk and soon took the one flight of stairs up to his apartment. The door was unlocked, as he expected.

"What's up in here?" he asked the two very young Indonesian girls busy grooming three macaws.

They both nodded and smiled, not really understanding what he had said. They knew what was expected of them, and made sure it was done. If they wanted to stay in Waikiki, Hawaii, America they did exactly what was expected of them.

The Parrot Master took a moment to look at the birds and smiled. These girls were quite industrious. The birds looked great. And, the fact that they worked in the skimpy outfits he had bought them was a nice bonus. All this for room and board, what a deal!

"Angkasa," he said pushing the suitcase toward her. "One more, clean clean, OK?" The older girl nodded.

"Aru," the Parrot Master said, sitting down heavily in the one decent chair in the place. "My feet," he pointed. "Massage plenty good."

The younger girl glanced at her sister who silently nodded. It was OK, she indicated. They both knew it. One day they would be free.

~~~

Our big Polynesian Hospitality bus pulled up to the Ohana East on the expansive corner of Kaiulani and Kuhio. It was off the beach, off the Ala Wai canal, but a bargain at under a hundred dollars a night for Kama'aina folks like us with a State of Hawaii driver's license.

The local girls at the check in counter were friendly and once they heard the Joy Strummers start a little song in the lobby got us upgraded to the Penthouse suites on the fourteenth floor. Of course it was really the thirteen floor but they called it the fourteenth to avoid the superstitious crowd. Unfortunately, the superstitious crowd had figured out that the floor right above the twelfth was really the thirteenth no matter what you called it. The entire floor was open.

Ma and Pa got a two room suite, as did Sandy and I. It was more than we needed of course, but at this height above Waikiki, the more windows the better. Pat and the Joy Strummers filled the remaining rooms and, since we appeared to have the entire floor, left their doors open. Ladies scurried from one room to the other, checking out each other's views.

Sandy and I closed our door after a moment and pushed the queen sized bed up to the huge picture window looking west.

"I think this may be a sunset to rival any on Maui," Sandy said, lying on the quilted cover. "Don't you think?"

Taking all of two microseconds to join her I laughed a little. "Of course, it only looks good bouncing off your beautiful face honey!"

She soaked up the compliment for a moment. "Come here liar!" and grabbed my shirt and pulled me in for a kiss.

I was falling over a cliff, again. Her lips said things to me I had only heard from her, silently telling me she was in love. Her hands played in my hair as I pulled her tightly to me, tucking one of my feet behind one of hers.

This sunset was about to be missed by at least two people, or so I thought, until the knocking on our door started.

"Hey, what's going on in there?" Pat asked, laughing along with several of the ladies.

Sandy smiled so hard it broke our kiss. "I guess the kids want to play."

"Yeah, but the playground is taken."

The knocking continued followed immediately by more laughter. I tried to ignore them but Sandy started laughing too and when the ukuleles began serenading us I went to the door.

"Come on in ..." I bowed and swept my arm toward the room.

"Why, thank you!" Pat said. "We haven't checked out the view in your room yet."

I turned to wink at Sandy. "It's spectacular for sure."

It appeared Pat had brought the entire crew into our room, wanting to say something to us. Sandy brushed back her hair and pushed me into the middle of the group in our expansive main room.

"Look you two," Pat began. "We know you're here to find Tiwaka, and we are all here to sing and play music."

Emma Jane stepped forward, her kukui nut and diamond (or was it diamonds?) necklace resting quite happily on a new blue and white mumu. "Perhaps we can assist? Just now, on my balcony across the hall, we were playing one of our new songs and quite a few birds gathered on the railing."

All of the ladies giggled and laughed at that. They commented to each other at just the mention of what they had seen.

"So cute!"

"Are all birds in Hawaii so wonderful?"

"Even the pigeons enjoyed it ..."

"Ladies," Emma Jane politely interrupted. She waited a moment and then continued. "We thought it a good idea after seeing those birds to ask you what Tiwaka's favorite song might be."

A chorus of guesses murmured through the group. *Blue Hawaii* by Elvis, or maybe *Tiny Bubbles* by Don Ho.

I looked at Sandy who had the same expression on her face that I no doubt had on mine. Pa stepped forward from behind Ma and raised his hand.

"*White Sandy Beach*," he said. "I've seen him pick it out of our playlist several times. But," he added. "It's the version by Israel Kamawiwo'ole, that nice kid from Kaimuki."

Emma Jane perked up at that suggestion. "Ladies, we know this one don't we? Remember when we were practicing songs from the band *Makaha Sons of Ni'ihau?*"

Everyone nodded.

"Our thought," Emma Jane continued. "is that if we stroll through Waikiki, singing Tiwaka's favorite song, perhaps he will hear it and find *us!*"

"That's a great idea, Emma Jane!" I said, getting excited that a viable plan was actually coming into focus. Prior to that suggestion I was just going to walk up and down every block in Waikiki and hope to get lucky. I might still do that, but their idea was far smarter.

Pat raised his arms as a conductor and prompted the Joy Strummers to raise their ubiquitous ukuleles. "And a one and a two ..."

~~~

Tiwaka watched in mild terror as the zipper opened above him, piercing the darkness of the suitcase with the ugly light of fluorescents.

"Apakah itu menggigit saya?" Angkasa asked her younger sister.

"Saya rasa tidak ada, dia terlalu tenang," Aru replied.

"Hey!" The Parrot Master barked. "English!"

Aru continued kneading the old man's feet, speaking softly. "She is afraid the bird might bite her, but I told her he won't. He is too quiet."

The Parrot Master sat up in his chair quickly, but not enough to keep Aru from her massage. "Is that bird dead?" he demanded.

Angkasa peered inside the half opened suitcase.

"Angkasa, apakah hidup?" Aru asked.

Angkasa put her arm half way into the suitcase, smiling. In a moment she pulled out Tiwaka, blinking his eyes rapidly and shaking his head slowly.

The Parrot Master leaned back in his chair, happy that his most recent investment was still viable. His head reclined again and he closed his eyes, content with the world.

"Aru!" he barked with a sneer. "Get the oil."

~~~

White Sandy Beach

"You'll need to learn a few chords, too," Emma Jane told me, handing me a spare ukulele.

I hadn't touched an uke since my small kid days at Haiku Elementary School, where it was a mandatory class. It felt comforting to have one in my hand again, almost as if those carefree moments of my history had snuck up and given me a hug.

It was difficult to remain worried or sad with so much happiness in the room. They didn't call them the "Joy" Strummers by accident. Yet, it was those deep memories, of Haiku Elementary and a young Tiwaka, that challenged my ability to keep my smile genuine. I sat the ukulele down on the nearest counter. A quick retreat into the bathroom to wash my face with warm water helped me. I had to gather all of my appropriate masks which I hoped I might wear with some success.

Emma Jane and Sandy met me at the door on the way out.

"Are you OK honey?" Sandy asked. Emma Jane was watching me closely right behind her shoulder.

"Uh, give me a moment..." and I ducked back into the safety of the bathroom. More warm water to my face, shaky fingers combed my hair and I took several deep breaths.

"Cowboy up, dude!" I admonished myself. The mirror seemed to give me some armor. Thank goodness it couldn't see below my skin. Feeling a little stronger after a minute I opened the door again. They were gone, vanished into the singing mass of the newest Israel Kamakawiwo'ole fan club.

As I walked past the kitchenette a ukulele appeared from the doorway there, held by a thin lady like arm. "Cowboy up," the elderly voice said. "Tiwaka's gonna need you."

Taking the ukulele I moved past the doorway to see a smiling Emma Jane. She winked and moved past me to the group.

I could do this. All I needed was a support group, and it appeared I had stumbled into a great one. And they could sing, too!

~~~

"Put the shackle on that one," the Parrot Master commanded Angkasa. "He's new in town and might think it best to go home."

Aru translated for her older sister, who reached down to the floor and picked up a parrot sized cuff, attached to a chain that snaked out from under the rattan couch she sat on.

He stood up after Aru had wiped the last of the excess oil off his feet. She had already slipped fresh socks on his feet and slid his shoes back on.

Walking into the only other room in the apartment he returned with a rolling dog cage similar to those used as airline cargo carriers.

"Put those three in here, it's time to shine on Kalakaua!"

It was one of the few times the sisters saw the man smile.

The Parrot Master loved his job and the thought of going to work fired him up. All those lovely young tourist girls oohing and aahing at his birds. They posed with the parrots as if they were really posing with him. At least that's how he saw it. It was a good fantasy and one that paid him instead of most fantasies in Waikiki that required you to pay someone else.

The two sisters secured the three macaws inside of the dog carrier, untwisted the leash he pulled it with and together carried it down the one flight of stairs to the sidewalk below.

The Parrot Master checked his outfit in the small mirror on the back of his apartment door before descending to the street below. He found his white curly hair framed his face quite nicely, but there appeared nothing he could do about his teeth. Nothing that he could afford now anyhow. Adjusting his red bow tie to perfection he winked at himself, and then winked again with the other eye. The girls always loved that one!

What the Parrot Master refused to acknowledge was that the girls that loved that couldn't have cared less about those little tricks, fifty years ago. However they had found his handsomeness magnetic. The problem was that he still thought he was a player, and those girls were long gone.

The mind can play tricks on the vain more easily than the modest. The Parrot Master had been young and living in Waikiki fifty years ago. So, how could he still not be attractive if he was still in Waikiki? The young girls still looked enticing, what could have changed? It would always be the free-loving 1960s in his mind, even if the calendar continued to lie.

It was one of the sad consequences of living in the tropics. Clocks were an aberration.

~~~

"OK, everyone, let's review, shall we?" Emma Jane waited for me to bring my ukulele up.

"F is our first chord. Strum it four times."

We all did that. I remembered enough from school to fall back into the chords easily.

"OK, now B flat, once," Emma Jane coached.

"Now, B flat minor, once."

"OK, good. C 7, once."

"C, once, then we start all over again."

After a few more tries I think I had it, at least enough to hang with the ladies.

Pat stood up from leaning against the lamp table. "Now, let's get the words down girls."

He began strumming the initial F chord and started to sing.

"I saw you in my dreams
We were walking hand in hand
On a white, sandy beach of Hawaii
We were playing in the sun
We were having so much fun
on a white, sandy beach of Hawaii

The sound of the ocean
soothes my restless soul
The sound of the ocean
rocks me all night long

Those hot long summer days
Lying there in the sun
on a white, sandy beach of Hawaii

The sound of the ocean
soothes my restless soul
The sound of the ocean
rocks me all night long

Last night in my dreams
I saw your face again
We were there in the sun
on a white, sandy beach of Hawaii"

Pat's voice was perfect for ukulele ballads and this one fit him like he had written it. The second time we tried it the ladies came in an octave higher and added a crystal like edge to his baritone.

Ma and Pa were old hands at the ukulele and were strumming in time with everyone else. I tried to keep up as best I could and that involved skipping notes when I got behind. Sandy made no attempt to learn the instrument in one evening and glided over to the middle of the room to dance hula.

On the fourth rendition, Emma Jane changed the words slightly. She wanted us to sing this version as we made our way around Waikiki in the morning.

"I saw **Tiwaka** in my dreams
We were walking **wing to wing**
On a white, sandy beach of **Waikiki**

We were playing in the sun
We were having so much fun
on a white, sandy beach of Hawaii

The sound of the **ukuleles**
soothes my restless soul
The sound of the **Joy Strummers**
rocks me all night long

Those hot long summer days
Lying there in the sun
on a white, sandy beach of Hawaii

The sound of the **parrots**
soothes my restless soul
The sound of the **ukuleles**
rocks me all night long

Last night in my dreams
I saw **Tiwaka** again
We were there in the sun
on a white, sandy beach of **Waikiki**"

Even the ladies got a tear or two at these new words, and I might have had a couple flood my eyes just a little. It worked well though, and by ten that night we all had the song down.

Pat and the Joy Strummers made their way back to their suites hugging Sandy and I one more time. Ma and Pa lingered a moment after the last of the Texans moved beyond view.

"Thank you Ma, you too Pa," I said, a little weary in my voice.

They both gave Sandy and me hugs and went toward the door. Ma stopped short and turned.

"Don't you worry now. Tonight Tiwaka will find himself a nice comfortable spot to bed down for the night. Birds do that you know. He is a strong confident critter and is obviously a survivor."

I nodded, keeping my voice silent unless it embarrasses me with a break.

"This town ain't got nothing on that bird," Pa proclaimed, a bit of proud sneaking past his smile.

They both entered the hallway and started down toward their suite.

"By week's end …" Ma said out loud for everyone to hear, her fist up in the air. "… Tiwaka will be the mayor of this burg!"

~~~

Street Life

For Aru this was her favorite time of day. Whenever the Parrot Master pulled his little cage of birds toward Kalakaua avenue and an evening of photography she was on her own. Or more precisely she was on the prowl.

All she needed was a boyfriend that could rescue her, and maybe her sister, from this indenture. Of course, finding a boyfriend that would feed and house them while ignoring their illegal immigration status might prove a little tricky. Angkasa though was going to be a tough sell to any young man. She was a beautiful person, but only on the inside. On more than one occasion people had asked Aru who her *brother* was. Angkasa kept her hair cut like a boys, had a semi-permanent scowl and was a little overweight. It didn't help either that her voice was deep.

The Parrot Master had taken them in only hours after their initial ride to Hawaii, a longline fisherman from Tavarua, threatened to sell them into prostitution. Aru had promised him sex in return for smuggling her and Angkasa into Hawaii from Jakarta, where, coincidentally, they had been prostitutes. Aru feigned seasickness the entire three weeks on board, unable to consider the fat fisherman and he was furious now that she had refused him all the way to Honolulu.

Poor Angkasa had fulfilled that promise to the fisherman, unbeknownst to Aru until much later. Still the man had wanted the pretty girl.

The Parrot Master had been cruising the docks at Aloha Tower for just such an opportunity. Boat people came in all flavors but usually shared a common affiliation with desperation. He could smell it across the water, docks or streets of Waikiki.

When the fisherman was throwing their bags onto the dock, cursing in some foreign language and spitting, he saw the two girls and had his mark. Quickly he walked up to the smelly trawler and waved a hundred dollar bill at the fisherman.

"I take them to the police for you? OK?"

The fisherman only understood "police", "OK" and the US currency. He looked at the two girls literally shaking in fear, figured he had had his jollies with the fat one and nodded, taking the money.

The Parrot Master quickly approached the girls with the demeanor of a policeman. They didn't know any better at the time.

"Do you speak English?" he asked them.

Aru nodded yes. Angkasa looked at her.

"Good then. I am a fair man. Instead of taking you to jail, I will take you to a safe place. You can sleep there. I will feed you, both of you," he said looking at the ugly sister. "You then must help me with my birds."

"Birds?" Aru asked, anxious to get off the dock and away from the fisherman.

"Yes, I raise parrots for the tourists. You take care of them and the police will never take you to jail." He looked at Aru firmly and held out his hand for her to shake.

Aru had already made a deal with the devil for a boat ride and now felt she was making another with his brother. She looked at Angkasa and translated the situation. She nodded and half looked back at the trawler, shaking off another pound of disgust with her shoulders.

Aru shook the Parrot Master's hand, feeling a certain coldness in his skin. His eyes, though, held a considerable amount of warmth, at least she hoped it was that and not the similarly appearing look of lust.

"Grab your bags, then." The Parrot Master looked over to the fisherman, still standing there watching, and half saluted him. "Follow me," and he marched off toward the bus stop.

Now Aru was standing at a bus stop again, but had no intention of getting on one. She watched only for those that got off. Her hair was pulled back in a sweeping ponytail accenting her angular good looks and big black eyes. She had shoplifted a nice yellow sundress that played favorably with her breasts and hips and let her long legs yell for attention.

A city bus approached, its blinker on and its tires hugging the curb. It stopped right in front of her. The driver immediately recognized her gig and nodded with a sly smile. If he wasn't working, he thought he might talk to her.

Several dozen people were already making their way down the stairs to the sidewalk. The old people always got off first and they usually gave her disapproving looks. Of course they would, Aru thought. They were jealous. What did they have anymore? A few coins in their pockets? She had the magic of firm flesh and a quick smile. Money couldn't buy that. But, she laughed to herself; they could rent some of it.

Some college girls got off next, too busy texting to pay her any attention. Just as well, they would despise her as well as some sort of virtual competition for the men in town.

Finally, Aru noticed, someone interesting. Actually two of them. Sailors, in uniform no less! Perfect she thought. She thanked her bamboo spirit god for such continued good luck. It was a difficult god, never making anything easy, but giving them what they needed, when they needed it.

The first sailor saw her before he even got to the sidewalk. His dumpy shipmate almost bumped into her before he did.

"Well," the first sailor exclaimed. "Ah loooow ha, baby!"

Aru smiled demurely and waited. He had all the signals he needed to proceed.

"Who's this Chuck?" the second sailor asked, a little irritated that they were still standing on the curb and not making double time to the bar.

"This, my fine friend, is ..." he held his hand out in introduction.

"Aru," she said taking a couple of steps back off the sidewalk toward the Parrot Master's apartment.

"Ah roo!" Chuck confirmed. "So nice to meet you, here. On the sidewalk. At the bus stop." Chuck smiled slyly. This wasn't his first port of call.

"Do you want to party bigtime?" Aru asked quietly. "My sister and I love to drink beer with you."

"Hey, Joe, you got that? She's got a sister too!"

Joe grinned. He had heard "beer", saw his buddy picking them up a couple of girls and they hadn't spent a dime yet. Honolulu was great!

"Joe can buy the beer, yes?" Aru said, gently taking Chuck's hand. "I'll show you where I party."

Chuck was smitten. He always attracted the pretty prostitutes, something he was subconsciously proud of. He found himself being pulled up the stairs.

"Hey, Joe, we'll be right up here. Get a twelve pack!"

Joe made a mental note of where they were, turned until he could spot one of the ubiquitous ABC stores and saluted his friend. "Roger that!"

~~~

Tiwaka heard voices coming up the stairs. At first he was worried that more bad guys would come to take him somewhere else, and he cowed a little.

Angkasa stroked his feathers to calm him. "No worries," she said, one of a few phrases she had learned so far. "No worries, birdie."

Aru walked in the room with her date, still holding his hand. She winked to Angkasa and turned to surprise Chuck with a kiss on the lips.

Chuck hardly noticed the ugly sister or the tattered parrot only a few feet away. His major thinking functions had been already transferred south. The only thing his subconscious verified was that there were no other guys in the room. With that potential threat nonexistent he easily flowed with the direction of Aru's kisses and tugs.

"Kau membawa satu untuk saya?" Angkasa asked. *Did you bring one for me?*

"Is your friend coming with the beer?" Aru asked her date.

"Oh yeah," Chuck said, slapping Aru playfully on her bottom. "He wouldn't miss this for all the beer in the world." Immediately Chuck thought that well, he might actually, for *all* the beer in the world.

"Anda adalah salah satu membawa bir," Aru confirmed. Yours *is the one bringing the beer.*

Angkasa immediately stood up, catching Chuck's attention for a moment. She ran her hands down her old dress, to send whatever wrinkles might be willing to leave on their way.

"Is that ..." Chuck turned back to ask Aru.

"Yes, Chuckie," Aru soothed her date's misgivings. "She is very, very good." She grabbed his belt and pulled. "Very, very."

"OK," Chuck said, knowing he would catch hell for setting up his friend with such an ugly woman. "She better be ..." he squeezed Aru's bottom again and pushed her toward the other room. "... very, very."

Joe dodged a second trolley crossing the street from the ABC store trying to keep the eleven remaining beers from spilling out of the hastily torn open twelve pack. He looked nervously for cops that might tag him for an open container. The odds were with him though, half a block and he would be upstairs with his buddy Chuck drinking beer and getting some nasty.

The sidewalk was thick with people now, all seemingly headed in the same direction, the other direction. Joe felt like a salmon headed upstream. If his luck held the analogy would play well with the spawning part too. He laughed to himself, no grizzly bears please.

The low rise two story apartments, circa 1957, were placed side by side right on the sidewalk and suddenly all looked the same as the one he had tried to memorize. Worse yet, there were some rough looking local guys hanging over the railings of some of them. Picking the wrong one could be a problem. They had already spotted his open twelve pack.

A loud bird shrill came out of one particular apartment, the one without a rough looking local guy. Joe tried that one, first putting an unopened beer can inside his fist in case he had to fight his way out. It was one of the best tricks he had ever learned, Throw a punch and the beer cushioned the blow on your own hand, and then when it inevitably burst, the bad guy thought his face had exploded. It provided a great diversion for successful escapes.

Joe walked up to the open door to see a woman's back turned to him as she bent over trying to get something out from under her chair.

"Chuck!" he called out. "You in here?"

He heard a grunt from the room off to the side and then "Yeah Joe, yours is on the couch." Laughter and another grunt followed that.

The girl bending over finally stood up, turned to greet him and held out Tiwaka in her hand.

"Aloha," Angkasa said, looking quickly down before she might see her date's reaction to her.

"Wow!" Joe exclaimed. "Cool bird!"

Tiwaka perked up at the attention, immediately liking his new fan. "Aloha," he managed to say with some effort.

Joe looked at the girl with the short hair, old dress and dumpy looks and smiled. He had eleven beers left to make her pretty.

~~~

Tiwaka had been around bars long enough to see a train wreck coming. Humans were so predictable! Anyone with a box of beer was trouble, regardless if they said he was a "cool bird".

And despite the fact that this girl had spent two hours grooming him and talking some strange language in soft tones as she did so, the weird vibe was strong. There was something else going on. Maybe it was the perfume.

She had done a good job, actually, repairing what she could and oiling the rest. Her scissors had trimmed the tips of feathers that were damaged and bent and her oiled hands had smoothed the rest into a nice coat of colors.

He knew exactly what the girl in the other room was doing with that guy and what this one wanted to do with the "cool bird" guy. Soon they would both be laying eggs for sure!

If only he had his tail feathers! He might then attempt to fly away. One small problem, though, was the shackle on his right leg. His attempt to break free a few moments ago had only landed him under a chair. Horrible things were there, surrounded in dust and scraps of plastic.

Tiwaka looked again at the ring of metal around his leg. Perhaps he could bite through it, or perhaps through that strange piece that overlapped the main piece. The chain was too heavy to mess with, and the end of it was somewhere under the chair, where he didn't want to venture again.

"Want a beer, honey?" Joe offered Angkasa.

She quickly took it, popped the top like a pro and chugged it quickly. Crushing the can with her one hand she threw it into the corner and held her hand out for another.

"Whoa there darling," Joe said, suddenly afraid he had not purchased enough beer. "One more until show time, OK?"

Angkasa smiled and pushed her hand a little closer. "Show time!" she repeated.

Joe felt better that she understood what he was talking about and gave her another. He popped his second and by force of habit did the math. Only eight left.

The action was getting louder with Aru and Chuck in the next room and an open door did little to mask the obvious. But, a ringing phone did.

Angkasa looked a little confused as to what to do. Usually Aru answered the calls since she spoke English, but she was, of course, busy.

At the second ring, Angkasa heard her sister curse but return right back to her moaning.

The third ring finally got Joe's attention. He knew better than to answer a prostitute's phone but thought at least they would. He tilted his beer toward the black phone on the table.

"You need to get that or anything?"

Angkasa looked at him with big black eyes and raised eyebrows. Joe laughed and finished his beer.

"Angkasa telepon!" Aru yelled. "Jawab telepon sialan itu!"

Angkasa stood up and went to the phone. She picked It up on the fifth ring.

"Aloha," she said almost in a whisper.

The Parrot Master took a moment to try and figure out who had picked up the phone, but the street noise was making it difficult.

"Aru, bring me the new parrot. We need another to Kalakaua and Uluniu!"

Angkasa didn't understand anything except "parrot" and "Kalakaua".

"Parrot?" she repeated absentmindedly. She knew the Parrot Master would now yell at her stupidity.

"Aru!" He paused a moment. "Is this Aru?"

"No, Angkasa."

Joe watched the conversation deteriorate quickly. If it looked like some pimp was on his way up he would have to grab Chuck, pants or not, and run out of there.

"Get me Aru! Aru! Aru!" The Parrot Master had no patience with the ugly sister; she couldn't even do a good foot massage.

"Aru, Dia ingin bicara." Angkasa said toward the open door.

Joe heard cursing from Aru and then from Chuck. Tiwaka and Angkasa watched the door to see what might emerge.

Chuck came out first, pulling his shirt down. "I'll take one of those Joe," he said. He turned to look at Angkasa, paused and then the parrot. "Cool bird!"

"Yeah, I know yeah?" Joe said. He popped his third beer, and feeling a little sorry for Angkasa gave her a third. Somewhere in the back of his mind he knew he only had five left.

Aru emerged from the room now, a sheet wrapped around her. Her hair was a tousled mess but she was glowing. She gave her sister stink eye and then picked up the phone.

"Yes sir, this is Aru."

She listened to the directions said OK and hung up. Turning to Joe she smiled.

"Sorry but my sister has to take that bird there to Kalakaua." She looked back to her sister and nodded outside. Turning to Joe she politely added "Maybe next time, eh?"

Joe and Chuck looked at each other and said at the same time, "Sister?"

Angkasa crushed her third can and threw it in the corner. Aru took note of where it landed but didn't care. Speaking to her in Indonesian she explained what the Parrot Master had demanded.

"OK," Angkasa said, standing and picking up Tiwaka.

Joe finished his third and stood as well. "I'll go with her!"

Chuck and Aru were a little surprised but thought it through one more step and liked the idea.

"Leave us a couple of beers will ya buddy?" Chuck asked.

"Sure." Joe handed Chuck two, Angkasa one more, took another for himself and sadly acknowledged two truths: that his last beer was now in his back pocket - and Angkasa was only half way to becoming prettier.

~~~

The street at 10:30pm was noisy, busy and brightly lit, quite unlike anything on Maui that Tiwaka was used to. Angkasa was carrying the chain he was still attached to with the same hand he was perched on. Her other was finishing that last beer.

Joe was tagging along trying to figure out a way to make this evening get a little more interesting. Getting out, and following this prostitute to drop off a parrot sounded good for starters. It would also give him a chance to buy more beer, which would be essential to him ending the night as previously planned.

Tiwaka was taking a moment to try and get his bearings. The bright lights were keeping him from seeing any stars and the moon was still hiding behind the clouds hugging the mountains in the distance.

Of course, escape had one big caveat. Escape to where? Tiwaka didn't see anywhere to really go. Concrete and glass towers stood guard over spooky little buildings with shadows full of cats and dogs and unknown monsters. The sidewalks were a stampede of humans, none of whom would step over a prostrate bird on the ground who couldn't even fly.

He had not yet seen one Tiki bar or even a beach bar. Cars and trolleys zoomed past, overtaking the mopeds and pedicabs in some bizarre contest of speed-racer. Competing luau shows at the hotels littered the air with music from every direction as if listening to a dozen radios stations all at once. It was exciting, it was warm and it was exotic.

But, it was also disturbingly strange. All the poor coconut palms had been severely circumcised *and* castrated. No coconuts hung under typically wide graceful fronds. It was all high and tight haircuts, fronds only at the top pushing up. Amazingly enough none of the people were barefoot and none were walking less than ten miles per hour. No one was even hitchhiking!

And apparently, unlike Maui, brassieres were not illegal. Tiwaka had always had an eye for that particularly interesting part of human females, something he had picked up as well at the bar. For some reason here, perfectly endowed young women insisted on not displaying their best feathers. Go figure!

Angkasa finally tired of carrying Tiwaka in her hand and placed him up on her shoulder. The view was far better Tiwaka noticed right away and so was the attention. People started pointing, both fingers and cameras. Flashbulbs lit off as if Paris Hilton were burning *her bra* on a Maui beach.

Now, this was better, Tiwaka felt. People was noticing how awesome he was! After all, "Photogenic" was his Hawaiian middle name!

Angkasa, Joe and Tiwaka rounded the corner onto Kalakaua avenue, the main run into Waikiki that takes some of the world's most fortunate travelers past the beaches and on toward Diamond Head. The excitement could be seen in the air, above the heads of the tourists, the gawkers and those working both sides of that street.

Several blocks ahead the Parrot Master was working his sales magic and Angkasa was a bit nervous that he would scold her. At least she could be sure of one thing, he wouldn't beat her. Not like the fisherman had, all the way across the Pacific Ocean.

Her date, Joe, seemed a nice enough guy, and didn't mind drinking enough beer to make them both comfortable with the inevitable.

As soon as she could dump this parrot she could get back to drinking with Joe. Maybe he would get hungry and buy them both something to eat. That would be nice.

~~~

Birds of a Feather

Tiwaka could hear them before he saw them. Squawking in some mix of alarm and frustration. Atop Angkasa's shoulder he could see the Parrot Master working a small crowd surrounding several tiki carvings. Each of those was crowned with a macaw that Tiwaka could sense was none too happy.

Flashes were going off in their faces and people were talking too loud, inanely asking them to say "hello". Kids were pulling on their feathers and the Parrot Master had a long stick he would poke them with if they complained.

His assistants, guys and girls just like Angkasa and Aru, down on their luck fans of the tropics, busied themselves working the crowd for credit card payments and upselling. One of them, Tiwaka noticed as they got closer, must be from Maui. Her bra-less sheer t-shirt and pearl necklace were featured in nearly every photo, a parrot on her arm and a customer on the other.

Angkasa noticed her too and felt a twinge of jealousy. This girl's blonde locks and trim athletic build let her earn more money all while keeping her clothes on.

"Whatever," Angkasa thought in the Indonesian equivalent.

The Parrot Master spotted them approaching and waved them over quickly.

"Look at this line will you?" he asked Angkasa, forgetting she couldn't understand him. "What a night!"

Angkasa could tell that he was excited and in a good groove. She nodded and smiled as she handed over Tiwaka, and his chain.

"Thank you very much!" the Parrot Master said to her, only glancing up briefly at Joe. He slipped her a twenty dollar bill and squeezed her hand as he smiled. He would easily make another hundred with the additional parrot. If he had another blonde exhibitionist he could make another five hundred.

Angkasa took Joe's hand as she took one more look at the blonde girl strutting her charms. She laughed, showed Joe the twenty and thought: 'with another twelve pack and the lights off she would be *that* girl tonight.'

~~~

"New guy! Thank God!"

"Welcome to paradise dude!"

"Where'd they dig you up?"

Tiwaka sat in the middle of the other macaws, his chain secured to a tiki pole similar to the ones they were sitting atop.

"You guys can talk?" Tiwaka asked, incredulously.

All three macaws took a moment from their wing flapping, squawking and other discomforts to look at the new guy.

"Are you kidding?" the oldest asked. "You can. We can."

"Two can!" the funny one chimed in. "Get it? Toucan dude?"

"Ha, ha," the grumpy one added, trying in vain to get his tail feathers out of the grasp of a three year old boy. "If we had beaks like that maybe we could dig a tunnel out of here."

Several cameras flashed at the same moment overexposing the birds in a burst of overwhelming light.

"Am I still here?" Grumpy asked.

"Yeah dude, for at least another two hours," Funny deadpanned.

"Where you from kid?" the older macaw asked. He was now sitting on the arm of the blonde.

Tiwaka took a few more moments to digest the fact that these birds were talking easily to him, and he to them. Just like the winged man in his dream, Gardner McKay and the hobo.

"Maybe's he's deaf," Grumpy finally said. "He sure looks like he could be ... is he missing his tail feathers?"

Tiwaka woke up at the mention of that. "Maui. I'm from Maui."

"Maui?" Grumpy continued. "That's funny. What brings you to this nightmare?"

Tiwaka looked at them and blinked. "A bad dream."

"Hey, new guy!" Funny said, now parked on the blonde's other arm. "Wake me up when it's all over, will ya?"

The Parrot Master was prodding the older macaw with his stick, trying to get him to squawk.

"In my next life," the older macaw complained. "I'm going to be the tiger that eats this guy."

"I'm gonna be the father of the eggs the blonde lays," Funny proclaimed, sitting on the head of red headed kid.

"Yeah, right!" Grumpy chimed in. "I'm going to be the caretaker that feeds you crazies old geezers oatmeal in the morning."

Tiwaka saw that these guys worked well together, even if it was as a chain gang. "Why don't you guys just ..." He stopped before he finished that silly question, feeling the shackle on his own foot.

"Yeah, well ..." the older macaw answered. "... I think you know the answer to that question eh?" He held out his wings showing they were clipped.

It was Tiwaka's turn with the blonde and he let the misery slip away for a moment as he got to inspect her feathers. He put his beak into her hair, trying to smell what part of Maui she might be from. The Parrot Master immediately got his stick up against his neck and pushed him back.

"She's not your type!" Funny said to Tiwaka.

Tiwaka turned to stare at the Parrot Master. First with his left eye to see the true intentions of the guy. Then with his right to see what dreams, if any, he might have. The Parrot Master was watching him closely as well, pushing the stick back over toward his neck while the blonde ignored the confrontation with smiles and wiggles.

The man was difficult to read. It seemed as if his true intentions and dreams were one and the same. A great combination except for the underlying premise: money. He was all about making money, regardless of how he did it. Tiwaka saw a dark history of selling endangered animals outside of zoos, smuggling drugs into school zones and human trafficking.   This guy, Tiwaka sensed in that brief insight, had killed, parrot and people alike.

Shivering for just a moment with this picture Tiwaka peeled these thoughts away so he could smell the Maui blonde's hair again. He had a scent of Lahaina at first, but then a distraction of Kahului mixed in with a touch of Hana. His beak moved deeply into her hair, next to her ear. She giggled and twisted her neck.

"She's from Hana!" Tiwaka thought just as the Parrot Master's stick bounced off his neck. "Hey, what's up with the stick?" Tiwaka took a deep breath to control his anger, just as he had been taught years ago. He also did something else, suddenly sensing danger. He focused, internally, and broadcast a message to the cosmos, a prayer if you will, asking for help.

"Watch out new guy!" the older macaw said just as the stick came down hard on Tiwaka's back.

The blonde dropped Tiwaka quickly and stepped aside, picking up Grumpy and turning toward a new set of cameras.

"Cower!" Funny advised. "Put your head down, now!"

The Parrot Master knew he had a new bird, who obviously needed some training and didn't hesitate to hit Tiwaka again, this time right where his tail feathers used to be.

"Don't move new guy!" Grumpy called out from the blonde's arm. "He'll stop in a minute."

Tiwaka was more stunned by the audacity of the attack than the pain. He stood still in shock.

"Good job, new guy," the older macaw coached. "Now, crawl back up the tiki to your post. We'll cover for you."

Tiwaka did as he was told, feeling the vomit move up his throat as a deep anger coursed through his entire being. At the top of his tiki pole he turned and looked at the Parrot Master again. He was taking money from a couple dressed like Hula Hattie.

The other macaws were talking to him, but their voices were drowned out in the noise of his own internal fury. Tiwaka swallowed deeply, forcing back the vomit, and his pride. This man, this Parrot Master, Tiwaka vowed, had won a battle, but would lose this war he had going with parrots. He looked at the three other birds, performing like circus animals. Winning, Tiwaka knew, required the orchestration of battle on the parrot's terms. Now that he knew the enemy's weaponry, knew the enemy's motivations, he knew where to attack.

"How many are there?" Tiwaka asked the others.

The macaws were silent for a moment, not quite understanding the question.

"How many?" Tiwaka demanded now. "How many other of us are under his control?"

The older macaw spoke up. "Twenty, maybe twenty-five. You'll meet them all tonight, after work. He keeps us in cages at his apartment."

Tiwaka began formulating a plan. He wasn't quite sure what it would be, but the first thing he already knew was that it would require all the enslaved parrots to act as one.

"All creatures suffer indignities," the older macaw said soberly.

"Yeah dude," Funny added.

"We all learn to live with them," Grumpy followed.

Tiwaka bowed his head and shook it back and forth slowly. "No, no." He raised his head high. "In the eyes of the universe this man is no greater than us."

~~~

It was almost midnight when Tiwaka found himself stuffed inside the dog kennel wheeling down the sidewalk. Funny, Grumpy and the older macaw were in the small box with him.

"Boy, could I use a stiff drink!" Funny said as they hit yet another bump in the sidewalk, throwing them all into the plastic walls.

Grumpy was looking out through the thin slits of the kennel. "It's him all right, not the blonde, pulling us along."

"Darn," the older macaw remarked. "I like the way the blonde puts us inside our cages."

All three of the seasoned performers echoed that sentiment.

Tiwaka had his beak pushed through a slit as far as it would go, trying to smell as much information as he could about their path through Waikiki.

"Hey, new guy," Funny said. "Whatchaya doing? The blonde went the other direction."

Tiwaka appreciated how these guys handled their situation and admired them for it. But, he sure didn't want to come to that point in his future.

"Are the other birds being taken back to the Parrot Master's apartment as well?" Tiwaka asked.

"Yes, most of them are probably already there," the older macaw said drearily.

"Have you been there yet new guy?" Funny inquired.

"I think so," Tiwaka said, still looking outside. "Are there two girls that live there with him, helpers of some sort. Groomers?"

"That would be Castle Macaw, all right," Grumpy spat. "Did you see the cages?"

Tiwaka bounced off the wall as another bump in the sidewalk threw them around. "No, I was chained to the couch, getting trimmed and oiled."

"Is that where they cut off your tail feathers?" Funny sounded infuriated. The others moaned.

"No," Tiwaka found his footing again. "I lost them in a storm, the storm that brought me here, from Maui."

The three other macaws were silent for a moment. Finally Funny asked the question they all were thinking of. "So, you really *are* from Maui?"

Tiwaka turned and looked at all three of them closely. The look of anticipation was thick in their eyes.

"Of course, why wouldn't you believe that?"

Funny looked at Grumpy and then both of them looked to the older macaw. He spoke then for all of them.

"Maui is especially important to us. It's where we hear of a magical place in the jungle, a tiki bar, where a powerful macaw has created a utopia of peace..."

"... and happiness, and good times!" Funny added, finishing up for the older macaw as his emotions forced him to gather himself together.

"Maui holds a promise for all enslaved macaws," Grumpy added. "This place we speak of, some call it Tiwaka's Tiki Bar & Grill ... we call it nirvana ... it's where we all hope to go when we eventually escape."

"Or die," the older macaw said quietly.

Everyone in the dog kennel was quiet for a long time. The three performers took a moment to dream of a place they had only heard about, and Tiwaka was letting the shock wear off.

"This Tiwaka," Grumpy continued. "is said to have been born here in Honolulu but taken to Maui for his spiritual training. All of us working for the Parrot Master pray that we will be alive when the Great Tiwaka returns here to free us, free us from slavery."

"Hallelujah," Funny seconded.

"We're here," the older macaw said at the stairway, his voice full of a great sadness. He no doubt thought he would never live to see the prediction come true.

Tiwaka remained silent. He thought of what the winged man had said in his dream. Now he knew exactly who it was he was talking about when he said "They can soar, but some don't know how."

Someone came and picked up the kennel and walked it up the stairs to the apartment, banging it into the sides of the railing a dozen times.

"Aru," the Parrot Master barked. "Are all the other birds here yet?"

Tiwaka could see the pretty girl standing at near attention by the same couch where Angkasa had cleaned him up. Her hair was in a bun now.

"Yes, sir, these are the last of them."

"Very good," the Parrot Master walked over to his chair and took off his shoes. "Put these birds away and come back to me with some oil. My feet are in need."

~~~

Song Birds

Ma and Pa were up very early, knocking on everyone's doors to wake them. Sandy and I were already on the beach, before dawn, looking for Tiwaka before the crowds blurred our vision. Auntie Lois had met us in the lobby to angel-sit Baby Kiawe for the day.

Ma was knocking on our door for several minutes. Everyone on the floor was now standing outside in the hallway wondering how deeply we could really sleep. Right before calling hotel security, Ma thought she would call my cell phone.

"Thank goodness you answered. We're all outside your door, worried sick!" Ma exclaimed.

"What are you doing outside our door, Ma?" I asked, dragging out the confusion a little longer, like a errant child.

"Why son, we are trying to get organized to get out early and look for poor Tiwaka, of course!"

"Well then, bring everyone down to the beach with you. We're already here," I started laughing. "Sandy says put some sunscreen on, it looks to be a spectacular day."

Looking down as I waited on the phone, I pushed aside some newspapers at the bottom of a wall in some wild hope that a crazy parrot would find that a nice place to sleep in. I only saw a crazy mouse.

"OK, then," Ma said, exasperated with me already. "We'll meet you in front of the Duke Kahanamoku statue in ten minutes."

"Thanks, Ma," I turned to Sandy and smiled. "They're on the way."

A couple of retirees passed us quietly, listening to the headphones plugged into their metal detectors. I knew Tiwaka had a metal band on his left leg.

Tapping one of them on the shoulder to get his attention I asked if he had found any birds with metal bands on their feet.

He looked at me a little funny then figured out my real question. "You mean *dead birds* with metal bands on their feet?"

My blank stare gave him his answer.

"No, sonny, nothing like that." He looked over to his partner who shrugged as well. "Good luck though," and he went back to his sand, lost coins and the occasional diamond ring.

~~~

The amazing thing I noticed about Waikiki, specifically Waikiki at dawn, was its amazing similarity to other remote beaches in Hawaii. Naturally, I'm speaking as one who can ignore tall hotels almost pushing the coconut palms into the sea with their big fat concrete feet.

It was easy to ignore those things so foreign and simply sit there in the sand with Sandy and watch the empty waves roll in slowly, washing the sand at our feet just like they did on Maui. It looked just as intoxicating on any other of the amazing islands here in the middle of the third planet's most wonderful of oceans. The air was just as sweet and calm in the early light, the birds just as melodious and the message just as pervasive: you are one lucky s.o.b!

I had lived in Hawaii my entire life and you would think it would have become old and stale. Some folks got what we called "rock fever" where they were slowly going crazy trapped within the smallness of their island prison. I could sympathize but I couldn't understand it. Me, I could spend three consecutive life terms here, but I was guessing I would only get one.

"Honu!" Sandy suddenly said, pointing just a few feet out from where we were sitting. Sunrise was starting to sparkle the back of Diamond Head and still these turtles were the only ones in the water. Crystal clear water, I must add.

Sandy was already walking out into the water, and I instinctively looked for lifeguards or DLNR officers that would ticket us for "harassing" the animals. Fortunately, the only people I saw were the two retirees far down toward Ft. Derussy now.

My beautiful wife, her long black hair already floating in the water at her hips, suddenly dove under and began swimming out to the Honu. I walked in to my knees and kept a watch.

Sandy surfaced in the middle of the bale at the same moment the dozen or so Honu also surfaced for air. She spun around laughing, her eyes as bright with love as I had ever seen them.

She waved me in deeper. "Come, baby, Wailani is here!"

Wailani? Our own amazing employee from Maui? I thought of Coco immediately and how she too had been one of these amazing creatures of God's fantastic and imperfectly understood universe.

Both Wailani and Coco had displayed themselves to me, hinting at their alter-egos, but I had never seen them as their oceanselves. I dove in excitedly.

Swimming underwater, I could see Sandy's gorgeous legs lightly kicking up a little sand as she stood in neck deep water. The turtles were moving their flippers only enough to keep them buoyant and stable next to Sandy. Several yellow tangs crossed my path as well as a lone lobster heading back to the safety of a hole somewhere in the reef. I might have taken a deeper breath if I had planned better, but I pushed forward and soon surfaced inside the ring of Honu, clutching Sandy's body in a hug.

"Baby," Sandy said softly. "They have some information on Tiwaka."

I looked around at the dozen sea turtles and nodded to each as if I knew them. I almost felt like a lost astronaut being polite to the nice aliens who were going to point me back to Earth.

"Which one is Wailani?" I whispered into Sandy's wet ear. They all looked the same except for a few blemishes on their faces and scratches on their shells.

"All of them are, honey."

"All of them?" I asked. Aliens sure were an unusual bunch.

"Wailani, and Coco before her are post-individualistics. Their mana, their mojo if you will, can be carried among groups, not just a single creature."

I looked at Sandy for a long moment, trying to fathom that statement. Smiling, I knew she would explain it to me again later.

"Look," Sandy continued. "Wailani wants to talk to us …"

"OK!" I said, bouncing lightly off the sand bottom with my toes. "I'm listening!"

"Well, it works this way honey." Sandy took my hands underwater. "We need to take a deep breath, go under the surface and put our foreheads together, like this." She moved slowly toward me, as if to kiss me, but leaned her head in first so as to gently touch my forehead with hers.

"Got it?"

"Sure, I can do that. What if I need to take a breath?" What if Wailani had a lot to say, I thought.

"It won't be a problem, trust me," Sandy said. She squeezed my hands a little. "Ready?"

I nodded, took a really, really big breath and followed Sandy underwater. All that air had me trying to float, but Sandy pulled me down to just where both our heads were covered with water and then moved her head to mine.

I have to admit that in all my previous experience of talking with other species of animals, namely Ococ and Tiwaka, and the occasionally unresponsive humpback whale, I had absolutely no preparation for this.

As Sandy's head got closer to mine it began. The singing! When her forehead made contact with mine it was like headphones had suddenly been turned on for me. It was the sweetest music I think I had ever heard. Angelic, happy and in perfect pitch. Turtles! Who would have thunk?

The music soon evolved into some kind of chant, still quite musical but changing from a celebratory mode to one that more resembled a message. I opened my eyes to look at Sandy, but at this angle I couldn't see her eyes. All I could see was a broad smile on her face and then I noticed she was moving her lips in time with the chant.

I didn't seem to need to take a breath yet, although I would have already been scrambling to the surface if I had been under at Ho'okipa this long.

Female voices became recognizable now, several chanting in what sounded like a Hawaiian meme. Soon I could hear Wailani's distinctive voice, soft and reassuring. It came from all directions, from even inside my head as if in perfect stereo.

"Ocean aloha to our Maui ohana," Wailani greeted. "We appreciate your love for our fellow creature Tiwaka."

I guess Wailani spoke English for my behalf. Or maybe that what's I heard, and Sandy was hearing them in her native Tahitian. It didn't matter of course. When I found out this was indeed the case later I was only that much more impressed.

"Tiwaka is safe but in trouble," Wailani continued. The singing and chanting had stopped now. A light hum was moving through us. "He sent a call for help last night."

My heart raced and I found my fists clenching. I was ready to kick someone's patooty all the way to Ni'ihau!

"Tiwaka No Ka Oi," Wailani said, the others repeating it. "The force is strong with this one," Wailani added, no doubt playing into my Star Wars spirituality. Sandy told me later she heard "He is a great and powerful leader."

"Tonight he will lead a rebellion, but his enemy is great and powerful and has enslaved many like him." Wailani sounded as if she were almost sobbing now, but it may have been the bubbles coming from my slow exhalation.

Suddenly I heard Sandy's voice, as clear and poignant as Wailani's.

"Where is he, our little Tiwaka?"

There was silence for a long moment, and I felt like maybe I should ask as well. Apparently, I was expected to speak. I knew better than to open my mouth underwater, so I tried simply opening my mind, and asked, "Where can I find my friend, to rescue him?"

Sandy squeezed my hands and I felt her happiness that I had participated.

Wailani continued as the others began a light chanting again. "He is on the streets at night, that is all we know."

I knew the "streets" meant he was vulnerable. The streets in any town, even Honolulu, were no place to live. I was ready to surface now and get on the trail. Sandy held me in place for another moment.

"Mahalo Wailani, so very, very much!" Sandy said, in a hauntingly similar singing voice to the Honu. She then grasped my hands and rose to the surface.

My lungs only then felt as if they had been missing air longer than they were used to. I literally gulped big air, in large 48 ounce portions. Sandy turned and watched as the turtles swam away. Some of them moved along the shoreline toward Diamond Head and some the opposite direction. A few headed out to the surf, a hundred yards out to sea.

I turned to head back up to the beach and saw the entire crew of the Joy Strummers standing there watching us! Ma and Pa were at the water's edge.

The surprise on my face was only matched by that on Pat's and the Joy Strummers. Apparently they had watched us underwater, inside a circle of turtles, something rarely seen in Texas.

Sandy joined me on the beach, both of us still standing at the water's edge. I didn't know what I should say or how much I should explain, so my CIA training kicked in and I just kept my mouth shut. No one was talking, and that was starting to get uncomfortable. The ladies were watching the turtles swim away and then looking back to Sandy and me, as if we might try and discreetly shed our shells and flippers while no one was looking.

Ma walked down and took Sandy's hand, both of them walking up to the group standing in the dry sand.

Pa came down and put his arm around my shoulders.

"Did you get any leads son?" We walked up the sand as well.

"Sure did, and boy I'm so angry, Pa, I could kick someone."

Pa squeezed my shoulders and then whispered so that no one else would hear us. "The cavalry is here now, we're gonna find him."

Sandy held her hands up to get everyone's attention.

A few of the ladies were still looking back and forth between the retreating turtles and Sandy, but most everyone else focused on her now.

"Everyone, Tiwaka is somewhere on the streets. So, let's start with Kalakaua, work our way down to Kapahulu by the zoo, up to the Ala

Wai and down by the canal. When we get to McCully we can split into smaller groups."

A few murmurs went up from the crowd and Pat was still scratching his head and still looking out to sea.

Sandy looked over to me and I shrugged. I couldn't imagine what she would tell them but I was willing to let her try something.

"I think you all noticed the Honu, the Hawaiian green sea turtles we were swimming with." Now she had everyone's full attention.

"Tiwaka was always a big fan of turtles, have you ever seen his Honu tattoo?" Sandy smiled. I got the joke but I don't think anyone else did.

"Anyhow, we thought it, I don't know, inspirational If we could swim out to those turtles and kind of pick up a vibe," she looked at everyone closely, trying to see if her story was making any sense, or progress.

Pat raised his hand.

"Yes, Pat?" Sandy responded.

"How did you get them to encircle you like that?"

Sandy looked over at me and laughed politely. "Well, you know, my honey there ..." she pointed at me. "He seems to keep French fries in his pockets days after a visit to McDonalds."

People started laughing at that, loosening up a little.

"I know we're not supposed to feed them, but they got a whiff while we were swimming and surrounded us."

Sandy began walking up toward the hotels. It looked as if we had diffused the questions about whatever magic they had all just witnessed. I turned to Ma and asked why they weren't waiting for us at the Duke Kahanamoku statue, how they had found us a block away in the water.

"Why honey, your mama always knows what you're up to!"

Her smile was a little more than playful. It looked to have quite a bit of accuracy behind it as well.

"After I've had my coffee that is," she said, punching me lightly in the shoulder.

~~~

Stress is a funny chemical, yes a chemical. It floods your brain during overload, making sleep difficult. Once your immune system removes most of it you're so tired it makes waking difficult. Unless there are twenty-five macaws next to you singing prison songs together at sunrise.

Tiwaka stirred in his cage only because his cellmate bumped up against him as they all started singing. Opening first his left eye, and then a moment later his right, he looked around a room slowly bathing itself with the sun.

He counted twelve large bird cages, including the one he was sharing with another macaw. Right next to him three poor birds had to share a cage together.

"Good morning," Funny whispered, skipping a bar of the song.

Tiwaka saw that Funny was there with Grumpy and the older macaw, crammed into such a space that their shoulders were up against each other.

He turned to look out the open door and saw Angkasa sprawled out on the couch. Aru's feet, at least they looked like her pretty feet, were sticking out into the doorway from a chair close by. The Parrot Master was nowhere to be seen.

"OK guys," some macaw from across the room announced. "One more time, for luck! Joey, you got the rhythm again for us?"

A deep base 4-beat started from across the room. Tiwaka was up now and listening intently, it sounded a lot like Johnny Cash's Folsum Prison Blues from the playlist back at the bar. On cue all the macaws joined in.

"I hear the trolley comin'
It's rollin' 'round the bend,
And I ain't seen a cracker,
Since, I don't know when,
I'm stuck in Parrot Prison,
where he keeps beatin' me,
But that trolley keeps a-rollin',
On down to Waikiki.

When I was just a baby
My Mama told me, "Son,
Always be a good bird,
Don't forget to have fun,"
But I bit a man in Kalihi,
Just to watch him bleed,
When I hear that bell a ringin'
I wish I had just peed.

I bet there's free birds eatin',

164

In a fancy French fry box,
They're probably pickin' guava,
And ignoring all clocks,
But I know I had it comin',
I know I can't be free,
But those birds keep a-movin',
And that's what tortures me.

Well, if they freed me from this prison,
If that free trolley was mine,
I bet I'd move out over a little,
Farther down the line,
Far from Parrot Prison,
All the way to Maui,
To fly higher with Tiwaka,
Above a blue sea."

"That was great guys!" the macaw from across the room said. "OK, let's review any problems we had yesterday..."

"Geez, why do we have to relive that?" Grumpy complained.

Several others agreed.

"So," the macaw said. "The younger crew here can learn what works, and what doesn't." He turned to the cage next to him.

"Kawika, I heard you had someone pour water on you over on Lewers. Tell everyone what you did ... listen up guys ... this is great!"

"Yeah, well, this ugly little brat thought it would be a big hoot ..."

The room erupted at the word "hoot" with every bird there squawking uproariously.

Angkasa and Aru finally got tired of all the bird squawking. It was such a cacophonous wave of noise in the mornings! Aru got up and closed the door between them.

The birds got quiet a moment but let their breath out when they saw it wasn't the Parrot Master coming to beat their cages and scream at them to shut up.

"I love it when she does that," Funny said of Aru. "Have you seen the feathers on that one?"

Several agreeable sounds came out of the male birds in the room.

"Yeah, yeah," Kawika continued. "OK, I thought you guys would get a hoot out ..."

The room went wild again. Tiwaka turned to his cellmate who was coughing from all the squawking.

"What's the big deal with ... that word?" he asked innocently enough.

The bigger bird looked at him and shook his head in disbelief. "Dude, it's what *Owls* say all the time ... get it?"

Tiwaka shook his head no.

"No? Really? Owls are the funniest creatures on Earth. When they say that, in their accents and all, it's a crack up dude!" The bigger bird looked away for a moment and then back at the new guy. "Get with it!"

Kawika let the room calm down again before telling the rest of his story. "So, anyhow ... this kid decides to pour some water on my feathers, started right up at my head and had half a bottle on me before I got up the courage up to try and protest ... I tried something wild."

Everyone asked at the same time, even Tiwaka at this point. "What was it Kawika?"

Kawika pumped out his chest in pride. "I thought you might ask. Anyhow, I had half a pint of water on me so I did what I always did back in the jungle ... I shook myself real good." He paused for effect.

The room was quiet.

"It got all of them wet! They hate getting water shook on them!"

The room went wild again, squawking and cheering.

"Great idea Kawika!"

This time someone banged on the door that had just been shut. Someone screamed at them from the wall on the other side of the apartment. Dogs across the street began to bark in alarm.

"How you'd know to do that Kawika?" one of the younger macaws asked, adoration in his voice and eyes.

Kawika basked in the glory of his story another moment before adding, "Because ... that's what Tiwaka would do."

A chant immediately began:

"Great Tiwaka, Maui No Ka Oi!"

"Great Tiwaka, Maui No Ka Oi!"

They got louder and louder. Immediately someone started banging again on the door, more banging on the apartment wall and now a car alarm was going off. Dogs were howling across the street. They were loud!

Tiwaka couldn't believe what he was hearing. How could a bunch of macaws on O'ahu have ever heard of him or the bar? And how did the story get so wrapped up in mythological proportions?

A sliver of sun found its way into the room, bouncing off the dull metal of the cages. Tiwaka saw that many of the macaws in here had metal bands on their legs, but not all of them. He looked down to see his own and was instantly horrified to notice his name was prominently etched into the brass, T I W A K A.

Here was the Great Tiwaka in their very mists and he didn't even have any tail feathers! He sheepishly looked around at the hope flowing through the cages. They were slaves, but they had dream. Would telling them who he was dash those dreams?

Looking over at the cage with Funny, Grumpy and the older macaw he noticed the older guy nodding in time with the chant, but silent. His eyes were closed.

After a few moments they stopped. The macaw across the room spoke again.

"We have a new guy with us this morning, if you haven't already noticed. He's with Elvis there in the cage by the door. Everyone give the new guy a big round of howzit!"

The macaws greeted him with cheers of camaraderie, with a hint of sorry-about-you-being-stuck-here-with-us in their voices as well.

"He's from Maui," Funny announced to the group. "Worked with us last night with the Parrot Master himself."

"Maui!" they all sang out.

"Have you ever met the Great Tiwaka?" someone asked. Others interrupted any attempt of an answer by chanting again:

"Great Tiwaka, Maui No Ka Oi!"

"Great Tiwaka, Maui No Ka Oi!"

Tiwaka moved forward in his cage and up to the topmost perch. He wanted to say who he was, but didn't know how. Elvis, his cellmate, moved down to the floor of the cage to give him room.

"Guys," the macaw from across the room said. "Guys! Let the new guy say hello, already!"

It took a few moments for the macaws to quiet down. Tiwaka didn't know how to start, other than get right the point.

"Thank you for the warm welcome to ... ah, Parrot Prison," Tiwaka began. "I wish I could say I was happy to be here ..."

The macaws all applauded.

"Now ..." Tiwaka started. "... we need to escape!"

The room went silent .

Grumpy was the first to speak. "Yeah right, the last guy that tried a prison break ended up feeding the cats for dinner."

Several macaws murmured their acknowledgment of that story.

"We can get out of here," Tiwaka said. "I have a plan!"

"Funny," Grumpy said. "You don't look like cat food to me. And those missing tail feathers are not a good indicator of the success of your *last plan*."

"Let him speak!" the older macaw in the cage with Grumpy barked. "We need new ideas ... I, for one, don't want to die in this hell hole."

That quieted up Grumpy for the minute that Tiwaka needed to keep everyone's attention.

"Look, Kawika there gave me an idea just now. He said the humans hated it when they got sprayed with water. Right?"

No one said anything, but Kawika was anxious to get some attention again and said, "That's right, they hate that!" He turned to his cellmate and whispered none too quietly. "I invented that, you know."

"Right!" Tiwaka started again. "They hate something else we can do even more ..."

No one said anything. Tiwaka looked around and suddenly saw how downtrodden this group was. It was a sad sight indeed. They were getting dulled by their confinement.

"They hate it when we squawk!" Tiwaka shouted, bouncing on his perch. "They shut the door, bang on the walls, tell their dogs to bark at us, even honk their car horns just outside." A few murmurs began. Tiwaka ran with the momentum.

"We can squawk our way to freedom! We can make it so loud they bend down in pain, covering their ears. When that happens, we escape!"

"Not a bad idea," the older macaw said. "Not bad at all."

"We'll need a little help," Tiwaka continued. "Some humans that will pick us up in those trolleys and take us to the harbor. There I have a boat already waiting for us. To take us to Maui!"

The chatter in the room was growing. Excitement was building.

Tiwaka knew he almost had them, save for one more thing he had to say. He looked at all of them, directly, eye to eye. Then he said it.

"The Great Tiwaka would go!"

The room erupted in chanting again, louder than ever before.

"Great Tiwaka, Maui No Ka Oi!"

"Great Tiwaka, Maui No Ka Oi!"

The walls were getting banged on by neighbors again, dogs were going crazy barking and Aru or Angkasa was banging on the door. Car alarms all up and down the street were going off as well.

Tiwaka joined in for two choruses and then took a deep breath. A very deep breath. A breath that would prove to them all he was quite serious.

He stomped his feet a little, working it up from the very depths of his soul. His wings began to spread, Elvis had to duck under them, and Tiwaka's head went back, clearing his throat for the mighty bird call that would be heard all the way up into the green mountain jungles of Manoa.

Tiwaka let loose with an earth shattering squawk that overwhelmed those in the room, forcing them into a reverent silence. His chest beat under his feathers, pumping every bit of blood, every bit of energy up toward his beak and the heavens. Elvis noticed that his wings appeared to be fluttering under a great effortless tension.

Every cage was watching him in fascination; they had never heard a bird, a macaw or a jet engine make such a loud noise. It was bringing tears of joy to some of them, tears pulled from the fact that they were proud that a macaw, one of them, could exhibit such power.

Suddenly the door flung itself open with a fury that tore it right off its hinges. It fell to the floor.

The Parrot Master screamed at the top of his voice. Macaws for generations later would retell the story of how even this paled in comparison to Tiwaka's Great Squawk.

The enraged man took to beating all the cages with his stick, rattling the birds and even spitting on them. Yet, the Great Squawk continued, even as the other birds cowered in fear from the Parrot Master.

Finally, the Parrot Master figured out where the horrible sound was coming from and turned to Tiwaka and Elvis in their cage.

"Dude," Elvis advised, shaking with fear. "Quiet! He's gonna beat you to death!"

Tiwaka continued on the same breath, getting even louder, his eyes wide open with fear - and deep with courage.

The Parrot Master began beating their cage, forcing Elvis to the newspaper covered floor. Tiwaka flapped his wings a little for balance as the cage teetered, but continued his defiance.

"Who *is* this guy?" Elvis wondered and went to look at the metal band on his cellmate's foot. He took a long moment to digest what he saw, looked up at the proud bird, head high and wings spread and had to look back to the metal band a second time. His bird brain worked quickly. *He's from Maui, he speaks of freedom, and says he has a boat ready to take us away from here. Oh my god, it's true ...*

The Parrot Master was furious. He hit the cage multiple times but Tiwaka would not stop. Finally he recognized him as the new bird he had recently acquired, without any tail feathers - the one that obviously needed some discipline.

He flipped open the lock on the cage, grabbed the bars with one hand and shaking it violently, spilled Tiwaka to the cage floor on top of Elvis. Reaching in quickly he grabbed Tiwaka and thrust him down to the floor of the room. Tiwaka knew he needed a new breath now, in order to fight for his life, and stopped squawking. The room was silent for just a few seconds and Elvis spoke quickly.

"His name tag says T I W A K A!" Elvis screamed out to everyone. "It's Tiwaka! From Maui!"

The macaws all looked at each other in amazement, as believers must do when they see prophecy fulfill in front of their very eyes.

The Parrot Master turned to Elvis who to him was squawking pure noise, swinging his stick and knocking the cage to the ground. If not for Elvis' quick moves, swinging his hips this way and that, he would have been hurt.

Tiwaka checked his run over to help Elvis when he saw that his was fine. His eyes focused intently now as he stared down the Parrot Master. His wings were half spread and he was bouncing on his feet like a boxer. A chant from the cages started out slowly as the birds encouraged their man in the ring.

"Great Tiwaka, Maui No Ka Oi!"

"Great Tiwaka, Maui No Ka Oi!"

"Shut-Up!" The Parrot Master screamed. "Shut your beaks!"

"Free us and we will!" Tiwaka proclaimed. The birds cheered loudly at this but the Parrot Master only heard more squawking.

"You need to understand how to be quiet!" The Parrot Master said, swinging his stick at Tiwaka.

Quickly, he dodged the fast moving stick, hopping above its arch at the last moment. The birds cheered him on, now chanting at full volume again:

"Great Tiwaka, Maui No Ka Oi!"

"Great Tiwaka, Maui No Ka Oi!"

The Parrot Master was not a professional despot, but in anger all men taste evil. His primary thought now was to permanently cripple his provocateur. He swung hard again.

Tiwaka was up against the tables that were holding the cages and when he went to dodge this swing he ran out of room. The stick came so close he had to suck in his stomach as it went screeching by. It wasn't enough of a dodge. The tip tore off small belly feathers which then flew up into the air for everyone to see. They floated slowly through the rays of morning sunlight.

"Ha!" the Parrot Master snarled. "I'm gonna give you some serious training in how to keep your mouth shut!"

The birds were screaming now too, trying to be as noisy as they could, doing anything to distract the man attacking Tiwaka. The noise coming from the apartment was so fierce now that people on the sidewalk were stopping to look up to the second floor.

Angkasa and Aru were watching too, from the outside edges of the door less door frame. They couldn't see much, except a bunch of very upset birds and their boss/landlord/benefactor swinging a stick at something on the ground.

Tiwaka knew that if the stick connected with him he would be seriously injured. So did the birds in the room. So did the Parrot Master and he intended to make it happen.

Another swing was coming. Tiwaka saw it in slow motion, just like they taught him in Auntie Melita's Tae Kwon Do class back in Haiku. Speed your mind up, like they do with film cameras, and you get more frames per second, effectively slowing down the action enough to react better.

Immediately he saw the stick arching toward his head. He stepped forward into the swing and ducked. It went harmlessly over his head. Tiwaka squawked in victory and the birds went even wilder! But, the Parrot Master was a dirty fighter. His shoe came swinging in fast and low and scooped Tiwaka up off the ground, flinging him into the cages behind him.

Angkasa and Aru saw then who their boss was fighting … a little birdie! Aru looked to her sister with a look they both immediately understood. The two nice sailor boys Joe and Chuck were real sweet on them and said they could stay at their apartment while they deployed to Manila for a month. That was looking like a better and better idea.

Tiwaka scrambled up to his feet quickly, ignoring the pulsating pain in his back now. The eyes of the Parrot Master were cloudy with rage and Tiwaka would have to use that to his advantage. His evil ears no doubt were still operating well.

Spreading his wings to their fullest, a magnificent sight in and of itself, throwing his head back, but keeping his left eye on the mad man,

Tiwaka let go with a rapturous sound that would be known to generations of future macaws as the Great Squawk 2.0.

The Parrot Master bent over in pain, grasping his ears, trying to prevent the sound from piercing his very mind. The caged parrots saw exactly what Tiwaka had been talking about now. Between their fear for Tiwaka's life and the inherent excitement of battle they knew then that they had a chance. A chance for freedom!

Tiwaka's Great Squawk 2.0 was forcing the girls away from their door side perch and driving normal people yards away mad with irritation. The birds in their cages said, as the story went years from now with their grandchildren, that Tiwaka was so loud the glass windows were breaking. How could they have known that people on the sidewalk below were throwing rocks at them? It didn't matter, the fighting was fierce and their bird, their captain, the Great Tiwaka was impressive in battle!

As the small glistening pieces of broken glass showered down over the battlefield they caught the sunlight with their sharp edges, twisting and turning the brilliance against the Parrot Master. His next swing was distorted and slowed. It was the moment Tiwaka needed.

The Great Tiwaka watched the tip of the death stick begin moving toward him again. His muscles flexed into tight masses of power, his talons curled and his feathers, from head to toe, shimmered with the focus of winners. Music played in his mind, big band stuff, marching to victory music, 4th of July drums and brass! He saw what he had to do. It was time!

He turned his body a few degrees to the side, sucked in his breath and as the stick whisked close to his neck, he turned slightly and grasped it with all his might, with his impressive and extraordinary beak!

Flapping his wings immediately he managed to stop the stick right there, forcing a vibration up the stick so powerful it fell from the Parrot Master's hand.

The birds were going crazy with cheering! The Parrot Master went to grab the stick again, but Tiwaka moved it an inch away from his grasp. The birds cheered wildly at the enemy's torture.

"Give me that stick!" he screamed, rage forcing more and more sweat to pour from his skin.

Tiwaka stomped his feet, first his left foot and then his right, taking two steps toward the Parrot Master. The crowd, as the story would be told in macaw lore decades hence, were jumping up and down in their cages so enthusiastically that the cages themselves were leaving the tables.

Finally the Parrot Master managed to grab the stick but Tiwaka held on tightly. As he went to swing it again, Tiwaka clamped down with all his might, with all the force from all the molecules that called his body home.

The birds were hoarse from screaming, the dust from the struggle was now floating through the sunlit windows, decorating the air with flickering jewels of light.

Tiwaka caught the Parrot Master's eye just as he was pulling back on the stick and winked. The Parrot Master didn't know what to make of that but hesitated when he saw it. He paused to think, just a small microsecond or two of a pause. Tiwaka needed not a nano more and bit down on the stick, snapping six inches off at the end!

The birds, as the story would be told to future grade school macaws sitting at their history teacher's feet, went so wild flapping their wings that the cages actually began to get airborne above the tables.

The Parrot Master stopped and looked at the bird with the snapped off end of his favorite walking stick in its mouth. He was shocked into inaction.

Tiwaka spread his wings out to their full magnificence and spat the stick fragment from his mouth. It bounced loudly twice on the old wooden floor before rolling under a cage. A Ninja Master of timing Tiwaka let out a loud victory squawk and rushed toward the Parrot Master, head down and beak wide open.

"What the ...?" The Parrot Master turned in terror and ran past Angkasa and Aru on his way out the door. "Get them ready for tonight!" he yelled. Aru quickly followed him to the outside railing to watch him run down the stairs. "I need a drink," she heard him saying.

Angkasa peered into the bird room and smiled. Tiwaka was standing victorious in the middle of the ring, while his compatriots cheered him with thunderous applause.

She went to her sister at the railing. "Is he gone?"

"I hope so!" Aru said. "I sure hope so."

Back in the bird room, Elvis crawled free from his overturned cage, ran into the room with the girls, looked around and ran back in.

"Well?" Grumpy asked, speaking for all twenty-four caged macaws.

Elvis stood tall and extended his wings fully for the first time in many years. "The Parrot Master has left the building!"

~~~

Pat and Emma Jane led the band as they all strummed "White Sandy Beach" in perfect harmony all the way to Kipahulu Avenue. From there we all took a trolley ride around Waikiki for one full circuit to rest our legs, but not our voices.

Every time they passed Launiu Street, where Pat had actually grown up, they all let out a big cheer. Ma and Pa were passing out guava juices to the singers as their throats tired. The driver, an older man from Waianae was loving it! His tip jar was filling up with every half circuit as the other tourists all assumed he had arranged the live entertainment.

My focus was on the streets, the balconies, the trees. I even scanned the baskets on the front of bicycles in case this was some weird replay of *The Wizard of Oz* and the Wicked Witch of the West had my little Toto/Tiwaka hidden away. Nothing got my attention, though, nothing was telling me to leap off the trolley, run over to a ball of feathers and give it a big hug.

But, the morning was still young and the trolley had a lot of gas.

~~~

Good plans should always be considered as Plan B. The *best* options are usually ones that present themselves at the last moment to those flexible enough to take advantage of them.

Tiwaka, or the Great Tiwaka as he was now locally known, had intended to engineer the Great Escape in the evening when everyone was out of their cages and on the various street corners of Waikiki. All the birds were to begin their best imitation of the Great Squawk when they heard the first police siren of the evening. As the humans crouched in pain and turned away, they would all escape and make for the rendezvous point at the Hilton Hawaiian Village Lagoon. Those birds that couldn't fly would hop a trolley. When Tiwaka asked about any birds in chains he was told that was restricted to new guys only.

Angkasa and Aru walked slowly and carefully into the cage room, picking up the overturned one and helping Elvis back up off the floor. The girls felt a great deal of compassion toward these animals that they had groomed, doctored and fed for more months than they could recall.

Tiwaka had hopped back up to an open table, outside of his cage, as the girls moved slowly through the room. All the birds, at least the male ones, were cooing softly and watching Aru. Tiwaka had to admit, she did have impressive feathers. And her sister had a nice smile too.

"We're leaving," Angkasa said softly. "We leaving this crazy, insane place," she said more to herself than to the birds.

Aru nodded and smiled. More cooing followed her every moment.

As if Tiwaka needed any more validation of his greatness, Aru went to where he was on the table and began to stroke his head feathers.

"You are quite the warrior aren't you?" she said proudly.

180

"*We are all warriors*," Kawika whispered, enraptured by the gorgeous woman. His head feathers ruffled up, fluttering involuntarily.

Aru moved her hand down to the table where Tiwaka stood, extending her palm facing up. "Come to me, my brave bird."

An audible gasp went up from the caged macaws, as if their most powerful and exalted jungle leader was now going to claim his most beautiful bride.

Tiwaka looked up at Aru, first with his left eye to see her true intentions. They looked to be genuine. He then looked at her with his right eye, to better see her dreams. There he saw a thirst for freedom and … something else. He couldn't quite tell at first but as she lifted him up and carried him, he felt it. It flowed from her skin into his talons, and up to his appreciative smile. She had a heart full of love.

Slowly she brought him up close to her face. A big grin was gracing her beauty and the chants began from the cages again.

"Great Tiwaka, Maui No Ka Oi!"

"Great Tiwaka, Maui No Ka Oi!"

Angkasa began opening the cages, swinging the doors wide. The macaws moved slowly out, as if in a trance, the same trance that Tiwaka now found himself in.

Even as they moved beyond the rusty metal of their cages they stood in rapt awe of their Great Tiwaka in the hands of the exquisitely beautiful woman. He was indeed worthy!

Aru brought him up to her chest, hugging him softly against her magnificent feathers. She puckered her full red lips, dropping her eyes slightly. Macaw history would record this moment for eons as one of the great trans-species kisses of all time.

Her lips moved slowly until they mashed softly against his great and powerful beak. Every heart in the room was racing, but Tiwaka's was focused on not bursting. Spreading his wings fully and silently as she closed her eyes Tiwaka hugged her, wrapping his great expansive feathers around her bare shoulders.

They both held that position for what many of the macaws in the room thought inappropriately long, perhaps because jealousy was coloring their perception of time. Clocks *are* an aberration, after all.

Aru finally pulled away, as Tiwaka folded his wings back.

"Ah, you are indeed a great bird aren't you? A lover and a fighter!"

Grumpy and Funny, still in their cages, fell against each other, unable to fathom the scene any more perfectly. The older macaw found himself tearing up a little.

Angkasa finally released the last of the cage gates.

"You are all free to go!" she proclaimed. "Fly away ... to a better place than this hell hole."

Tiwaka thought there would be a mad rush for the door but looked down to the floor to see every last macaw lining up at Aru's feet.

"What are they doing?" Aru asked, sitting Tiwaka back down on the open table.

Tiwaka knew. Instinctively, so did Angkasa, who explained it to her little sister.

"They all want a kiss."

~~~

We had asked our trolley driver to alter his route to roll down different parts of the varied Waikiki neighborhoods. The Joy Strummers were the most angelic voices I had ever heard, if I didn't count the turtles. Pat was standing tall among them in the aisle, singing better than any since probably Don Ho.

Our driver had already paid for Christmas and his first daughter's wedding with the tips and at a red light turned to us.

"You guys are great! I'll take you anywhere you like go!"

We had just turned off of Saratoga onto Kalia and were heading for the back entrance to the Royal Hawaiian Shopping complex. But, there was a less traveled road just to our left called Beachwalk.

"Let's go slowly down this one!" I requested.

"No problem bruddha." The driver turned back to his windshield smiling. "You guys are hu'ihu'i!"

I had to agree.

"Let's all stand for this one ladies," Pat said as we slowly turned the corner onto Beachwalk. "*Come, and Rejoice with Me!* On three ..."

I felt a twinge of something as we moved slowly up the road, the first we had seen with no traffic whatsoever. I looked over to Sandy who must have felt something as well, as she was hanging off the back door step like those pictures of people in San Francisco.

Ma and Pa were moving with the music, swinging in each other's arms, laughing and smiling like newlyweds. I couldn't help but think it was them that had brought Tiwaka to me as a young boy, through some unfathomable amount of love - a deep and powerful love that I was only just beginning to feel with Sandy and Baby Kiawe.

I searched every coconut tree, every bush, every balcony lining the street, every corner of every shadow. I needed to bring my own child such a present as well, the same one they had given me. I had to find Tiwaka now not just for myself but for my baby, for my new family. I don't know what it was about that silly bird, but when he was perched between the vodka bottles singing or swaggering down the bar with a beak full of Brazil nuts he was ... hu'ihu'i - awesome.

We *needed* Tiwaka!

Tiwaka's take on the world was just what the world needed to keep it going day after day – hope. Hope that there would always be chocolate covered nuts under the counter, hope that a customer would drop a piece of fish off his plate while watching the hula dancers on our stage. Hope that one day, with a great deal of faith and effort, he would fly to the great heights of our amazing sky. Hope that in the quietest of moments, at the cliff's edge above the tool shed, he might still commune with his old friend Ococ. He was the personification of all that could be right with the world. He was my dearest friend, with feathers anyhow.

My eyes followed the coconut trees along the sidewalk up as they reached mightily up into the clear blue skies of Hawaii. Birds flew freely there, singing down to those of us below. The delicate white puffs that blew over from the green jungles behind it all danced on their way to the sea. They had hope as well; hope that those who embraced their creator would also enjoy similar miracles.

~~~

Aru and Angkasa had their small bags packed with the few possessions they had managed to accumulate. They followed the macaws out the door and down the stairs as they marched two by two to the sidewalk. The sisters held hands as well, like they had done so many years before, when the world had always smiled on them.

The sun was shining on their skin, warming them like it had back then. The brilliance glinted beautifully on Angkasa's black hair, shimmering as it washed her with light. She was ecstatic and began to giggle. She couldn't stop and soon Aru was joining her. They looked at each other, happy beyond belief that they were making the final change in their move from Jakarta to true freedom.

Tiwaka felt good that they had indeed escaped, but felt again the dread as to where it was they had escaped to. Buildings, cars and coconut palms with no coconuts! It was a strange world they now found themselves in.

"What now?" Grumpy asked, but without an iota of grumpiness in his voice.

Funny and the older macaw mistook his question for a complaint and gave him some serious stink-eye.

"I was just wondering," Grumpy confirmed.

"I'm going wherever she's going," Funny said, snuggling up to Aru's recently shaved legs. "She's so smooth ..." he cooed.

For a moment, to those that might have been watching the street below from their rented rooms, or through the windows of the street level waffle house, the scene resembled a parade team, before they spread out to move down the street. The two relatively tall women towered over their colorfully attired marchers. Of course, if anyone of those that might have seen such did so, they might have immediately asked for a second Bloody Mary.

"So, what should we do now?" Aru asked trying to politely brush Funny away from her legs.

Angkasa, the always resourceful older sister, looked to the street for guidance, and there saw one of Waikiki's ubiquitous free trolleys headed their way. She was feeling deeply inside her soul that something needed to work in their favor, wishing that some miracle might take them away from the degradations they had suffered, to a place where they could be happy again. She heard singing ... and the finest ukulele music ever played anywhere by anyone.

Pat's booming voice added the bass that the older ladies needed to really belt out their hymnal and with the ukuleles it was indeed a joy to be strumming with them. I tried to keep up, but just focused for a moment on the words.

> And now I know it all,
> Have heard and known His voice,
> And hear it still from day to day.
> Can I enough rejoice?

Tiwaka heard the music too, and the singing. It had been a while since he had heard such, since he had last been at the bar on Maui. He couldn't see where it was coming from, so he stepped off the curb and into the street.

The driver was looking back to the singers for a moment, taking his eyes off the empty road ahead. His speed was hovering around 5 miles per hour, his foot resting lightly on the brake pedal.

Tiwaka saw the big trolley headed toward him. Something told him to look closer, to open his mind to the possibility that there might actually be ...

Angkasa figured they could catch the trolley and at least get out of the general area. She stepped off the curb and into the street.

Tiwaka felt his mojo rising. He might have saved the macaws of Waikiki, but he still had to find his people. He stood tall there on the black asphalt, warming already in the mid morning sun. Instinctively his magnificent wings deployed to their full and mighty expanse, impressing several mynah birds watching the action from above. He raised his head high and with no small effort moved a Great Squawk up from the depths of his belly.

Angkasa stepped out into the middle of the road, just behind Tiwaka and raised her hand to hail the driver, just as the proud bird let loose his call.

The man from Waianae had been driving trolley for years and had never had quite the fright he felt shocking his old heart just then. With his head turned to the back of the trolley, even with his slow speed and foot on the brake he knew it was risky. The loud screech he heard vibrating throughout his trolley must be either be someone being dragged under the carriage or the bumper scraping the paint off an expensive car.

Turning to look quickly, as his foot pressed down firmly on the brake, he saw a young woman standing in the middle of the road, her hand held high. The confusing part, initially, was how could she make such a sound? He checked his mirrors quickly, but he was a couple of feet in the clear on either side. Maybe there was someone under the trolley?

The trolley lurched to a stop; he set the hand brake and jumped off the left side step to look under the carriage.

Tiwaka thought it strange that the driver jumped out of the trolley was so interested with what was underneath. No matter, he walked up to the side of it. Turning he looked to the twenty-five other macaws still standing on the sidewalk with Aru.

"Follow me!" Tiwaka said, waving all the birds over to the door step.

Angkasa went over to the driver and looked underneath with him.

It startled him when he turned and saw her face next to his.

Her eyebrows went up.

"No, nothing thank God," the driver confirmed to himself. He stood up straight, hands on his hips. He pointed casually to his trolley. "Do you want to board?"

Angkasa nodded and got on behind him.

Aru was stepping up to the other side, twenty-five macaws right behind her, boarding two by two.

If my memory serves me right it was Ma that screamed first. Soon after that it was Sandy, jumping up and down. Moments later the entire Joy Strummers were hooting and hollering.

The birds boarded, nodding to the driver as they passed him and moved down the aisle to our loud cheers.

As you might imagine, despite my lifelong love for Tiwaka I did have some difficulty in figuring out which one, if any, was him. After the initial shock of twenty-five macaws boarding our trolley, everyone else had the same question as I did.

"Tiwaka?" I said softly. My hope was tentative. Sandy immediately began looking at all of their feet, reading name tags out loud as she went.

"Geronimo, Jesus, Gandhi, Buddha, Elvis …"

Our trolley sat dormant on the pavement as we looked at every bird. Some didn't have tags, but were obviously too old, or too young to be Tiwaka. Finally, Sandy held up the last bird. She looked over to me and shook her head no, and began to cry.

"Tiwaka!" I said desperately. "Tiwaka! Where are you?" My heart was peeling away layers of fortitude, exposing itself to a terrible break.

I could hear my breath becoming more and more rapid. My palms were sweaty and my hands shook. I had to turn away from everyone as I felt a flood approaching my eyes. How could this be? Twenty-five macaws board our trolley, out of nowhere, and not one of them is my beloved Tiwaka. How could this …

Maui and Macaw mythology merge at this point, agreeing to the fact that it was then that the Great Squawk 3.0 was first heard. It was a happy squawk, one full of pride and relief. It was impressive in its volume and range, setting off car alarms along the entire road. Mynah birds were falling in auditory drunkenness from the trees and pigeons became so confused that they began dancing with the mynahs on the sidewalks. Surfers out on the reef break In-Betweens thought it was a tsunami alert.

I recognized that squawk of course, but only the inflection. The greatness that now imbued his tone was new. Running to the front of the trolley I looked out as Tiwaka tried again to hop up to the first landing on the door step.

"Tiwaka!" I cried. "Tiwaka, boy!"

I stepped down onto the warm black pavement and picked up my bird. He looked up at me, both eyes at once and smiled in a way that only those that have been around beaks for years can discern.

"I love you, boss!"

"Oh ..." I said hugging Tiwaka to my chest. "... I love you too boy!"

Turning to walk back up the steps I didn't care if my cheeks were streaked or that they were bright pink. It was momentous and I would never forget the moment, ever.

"Tiwaka!" I said holding him up for everyone to see.

"Tiwaka! Tiwaka!" all the humans began to chant.

The macaws began squawking as well, a coordinated sound that, to my ears anyhow, sounded a lot like:

"Great Tiwaka, Maui No Ka Oi!"

"Great Tiwaka, Maui No Ka Oi!"

I hugged him so tightly I had to pull away a little for fear of hurting him. That is when I saw that his tail feathers were missing. Actually, they weren't quite missing, but rather that new ones were growing where the old ones once were.

"Rough ride?" I asked.

He looked up to me and nodded.

We would talk later, now it was time to celebrate.

The Joy Strummers began a rousing rendition of something that had a lot of "Hallelujahs" in it. I didn't know the words, but every time the word "Hallelujah" repeated I yelled it out at the top of my lungs.

The driver started down Beachwalk slowly, and that's when we figured out Beachwalk was a one-way street. We had to move over so a KIA rental could go past us, its driver looking as if he had done the wrong thing.

"Oh well!" the driver said, turning sharply right onto Kalakaua and ringing his bell with his hand. He was extremely happy no one had gotten underneath his trolley.

We were all singing now and every macaw was perched on the window sills for the entire world to see. Tourists boarded, sang along with us and got off a block farther than they had intended to. We circled Waikiki for the next hour, picking up people and sharing with them our good times.

The driver made enough money to pay off his mortgage.

~~~

No Ka Oi

After some time we all finally began to tire and get hungry. I wanted to treat everyone to a nice restaurant I knew about at the Hilton Hawaiian Village. *Dellalicious* was the hottest family-style Italian restaurant in town and it seemed a good choice. Our driver took us over to the parking lot near the Lagoon, parked and asked if we needed him anytime soon. We didn't.

I watched as he walked briskly over to the hotel, to meet his wife who worked there, with the good news about the mortgage. Ma, Pa and the Joy Strummers were already heading out to *Dellalicious*. Sitting there for a moment with Sandy and twenty-six macaws I wondered what we were supposed to do with the other twenty-five.

"Can you believe it?" I asked her, enjoying the afterglow, Tiwaka on my lap and his twenty-five friends hanging out with us.

"Actually, I can." She smiled at me, one of those heart wrenching smiles that tells one you are blessed beyond belief. "And I know you can too."

I nodded. Sure, I knew. Luck came to those that pursued it. Make yourself available for good things to happen, they will. Still, sometimes, in moments of pure amazement I had to wonder. How? How could it all work out so well?

Paradise, I figured, came to those patient enough to let things work out the way they were going to anyhow.

While we waited for Pat to call if there were indeed tables at this popular restaurant Sandy and I watched the colors change slowly with sunset. The lagoon was empty save for a few lingering tourists on its edges. The grand hotels that lined the beach from here to Diamond Head were all busy turning on their sparkling lights and firing up their shimmering tiki torches. Music began wafting in on the gentle tradewind, hinting of dancing and singing and perhaps loving.

Sandy squeezed me tightly and turned to kiss me. Yeah, that's right! I AM the luckiest man on the planet. If only for this one instant, under her warm lips, draped in her long beautiful hair, I most certainly was. This moment, *today*, is really the only slice of time that matters. The future and the past were all interesting details related to today, but it was *today* that mattered, *today* that made any real difference in the world.

As usual I could expect Tiwaka to interrupt me when Sandy was kissing me, it was a special genius he possessed. It's what made him adorable. He was only craving attention. So, I thought this time was no different, but as I peeked out with one eye I saw what had attracted his attention.

A beautiful and relatively large schooner was sliding silently into the lagoon. It had to be over sixty feet and crewed by … maybe the one guy I could see at the helm. Tiwaka had already hopped off the trolley and was walking over to the water's edge. His twenty-five friends followed him at a King vs Commoners distance.

Sandy turned to look when she felt my distraction.

"Oh look at the Honu!" she said, somewhat in awe.

I noticed them then as well, almost as if they were escorting the great boat into the lagoon. Dozens of sea turtles led the bow into the still waters.

"Do you see the schooner, too?" I had to ask, as it appeared to pulse into my view and then fade for a moment. I blinked a few times to clear my vision.

"Yes, honey. It's a great ship, indeed." Sandy was standing now, asking for my hand, and we made our way out to where Tiwaka and his friends were standing.

We all stood there, the two humans madly in love with each other and a bunch of recently freed macaws, and Tiwaka, or rather the Great Tiwaka.

The schooner stopped mid lagoon and the one man on board threw a small dingy over the side, jumped in and rowed over toward us.

"Tiwaka?" I asked. "Do you know this guy?"

When he answered it was the first time I can remember him speaking so clearly, as if he were my own human brother and not a highly intelligent bird from a bar in the jungles of Maui.

"Yes, I do, in fact," Tiwaka said, looking at me. "He saved my life several days ago. He's here to take my friends to Maui." Tiwaka turned back to look at the man rowing up to the sand now.

"Ahoy!" the man said as he stowed his paddle and stood ankle deep in the wet sand.

I waved a little and nodded. Sandy walked up to him and gave him a big hug, putting her head on his shoulder.

"Thank you so much," I heard her say. "For saving our friend."

The man looked up to me and smiled, patting Sandy on the shoulder. "My pleasure entirely." He turned to Tiwaka.

"So, Tiwaka, my friend…" he said gently walking over into the midst of the macaws. "You have a job for me?"

I watched as Tiwaka hopped up into the man's hands and spoke to him just as clearly as he had to me only a moment ago.

"Yes, I do!"

"Ah, then matey, what might it be?"

"Well, my friends here …" Tiwaka said sweeping one of his large wings over their heads. "… they need a ride to Lahaina, if you don't mind."

The man, who I now noticed had a tiki token of some kind hanging around his neck, looked at the group of macaws.

"Can they tie a line? Or bail water, or fetch me a drink?"

"Oh yes, all of that!" Tiwaka exclaimed. "And more."

The man leaned back a little and smiled broadly. "Great, then I have a crew!" He waved the birds over to his dingy. "Welcome aboard!"

The twenty-five macaws quickly made their way onto the gunwales of the dingy and wherever else they might fit.

"Tiwaka?" I asked. "Introductions please?"

The man saw me then and walked over holding out his hand.

"Gardner, sir. Gardner McKay, Captain of the good ship *Tiki*."

His hand felt firm, his grip sure. I caught his eye for a brief moment, and then knew who he was. He was a man from another time, a man who was only visiting now. I wondered if I, at some point in the future, would be just such a visitor.

"Nice to meet you, Captain," I smiled. "How long to Lahaina?"

Gardner looked at his dingy full of macaws and laughed. "Best guess, with this crew? A full week."

Tiwaka hopped down and walked back over to Sandy and I. Sandy picked him up and put him on her shoulder.

"Well, then," I said. "We shall see you then, in Lahaina."

Gardner smiled and saluted. Turning he got into the dingy and with the wind power of twenty-five macaws flapping their wings at his stern made his way back to the schooner. Sandy and I watched as they boarded, pulled up the dingy and soon turned the great ship to exit the lagoon.

All three of us watched as the *Tiki* made her way silently out of the lagoon, narrowly missing some party boats that apparently didn't see her. Eventually, she moved into the distant blur of the horizon.

Pat finally called saying they had a table big enough for all of us. Sandy and I gathered our stuff from the trolley and made our way into the tropical splendor of the Hilton Hawaiian Village. Tiwaka was sitting pretty on Sandy's shoulder.

"So, Tiwaka," I asked. "When did you learn to speak so much more clearly?"

Tiwaka turned to look at me, squawked something that sounded a lot like a chuckle and said, "The question should be when did you, my brother from another mother, learn to hear me so much better?"

~~~

Two mornings later I found myself, my honey and my brother from some other mother sitting on the still cool sands of an unawakened Waikiki. The surf was a little bigger than six or seven feet and as often occurs here, was perfectly glassy. I was watching one particular break that had the fortunate habit of peaking just to the side of a nice deep channel and then peeling itself beautifully in the opposite direction. There was only one longboarder out and for some reason I felt no need to rush out into the water.

Tiwaka was sitting contently on Sandy's lap, looking up at her, and sometimes behind and up into the mynah bird filled coconut palms. I turned to look there as well, and it might have been my imagination - something I had to acknowledge as a large influence on my perception - but the mynah birds were all watching Tiwaka as well.

They no doubt had watched Mayor John Steinmiller present Tiwaka with a key to the city, for his efforts in freeing the macaws, or maybe they had caught the free trolley parade he led down Kalakaua avenue. I didn't think mynah birds could read, but who knows, they may have read Burl Burlingame's op-ed in the Honolulu StarAdvertiser expounding the virtues and economic advantages of better regulating our natural resources – including birds. No doubt they were jealous that the local Label-GMO coalition wanted to use him as their mascot. Posters were everywhere showing Tiwaka next to the recently freed macaws proclaiming they were now "Free to Eat Organic".

Everyone wanted to have their picture taken with him. The famous painter Kerne Erickson had even agreed to paint his portrait, an honor few birds had ever experienced.

Turning back to watch the surf, and that lone longboarder carve a turn into the crest before driving back down to setup for a nice barrel, I took a deep breath of the tropical air. It was fragrant with the mist of the sea and the perfume of plumerias just behind me.

Waikiki was stunning in how it managed to remain magical in the face of concrete, traffic and the likes of one Parrot Master. You could, with very little effort, feel the mana - the spiritual energy, in the place. It was in the sand where I sat, in the trees, in the surf and throughout the vistas of the entire Waikiki area. They all literally vibrated with it. Good or bad, Waikiki took what we gave it, what we did to it and turned it all into something inspiring. Such was the power of the 'aina – the land.

No Ka Oi came to my mind. Translated roughly as *the very best* and adopted by the folks on Maui long ago as their slogan I saw that it really applied here as well. In fact, as I let my mind go to all the places in Hawaii that I have had the honor of visiting it really applied universally throughout the islands.

Ah, but that was daydreaming. I broke my trance and looked over to Sandy. She was watching me daydream, waiting on my return and with a gentle kiss said, "Let's go surfing."

~~~

I inhaled the sweet smell of my strawberry flavored surf wax, pulling hard on my longboard with my arms as I had to race to keep up with Sandy. I followed her through the channel out to just beyond the break, trying to keep from focusing on her fine form or risk hitting the shallow reef. The waves were big enough to demand full attention and respect.

The sun was still nestled behind Diamond Head letting the clear ocean keep its purple tint a bit longer. When we reached our spot outside the break and sat up on our boards, I immediately looked down into the water. Habit or superstition, I couldn't say, but I always liked to know how deep the water was and if I was sharing it with any critters bigger than me. This morning, my eyes reported eight feet, and no.

I felt a little hesitant about leaving Tiwaka on the beach. He was wary about going out in the water with me on my surfboard. With all his recent trauma I didn't want to push him into anything he wasn't completely comfortable with. There was no one on the beach this early so I felt he would be relatively safe. But, I kept turning to look back for him – he was quite easy to spot against the sand. It took me a couple of gazes to spot him, as waves broke between him and me, but finally I saw him sitting on the short wall outside of the Shorebird bar. On either side of him I saw a dozen or more mynah birds. They appeared to all be watching us.

Sandy hooted, the universal alert about a set of waves approaching, so I quickly turned back to the business at hand. That lone longboarder was outside of where we were and perfectly positioned to catch the first eight footer. It stood tall and proud, pushing the still wind up to its crest where it tickled it with a feathering whiteness.

This guy took two strong strokes with his arm and stood to his feet just as the wave picked up his board from behind to hurdle it forward. His arms went out, like Tiwaka's might, and for that short instant of balance, we all feel when surfing big waves, slid down the smooth face. His entire body was extending from his tip toes to his finger tips as he approached the bottom of the wave, where he suddenly compressed in a bottom turn and turned to race the wall up ahead.

The wave's channel side shoulder was just passing under me before I had a chance to see the rest of his ride. From the looks of the back of the wave, he was most likely enjoying a big dry barrel ride.

"Wow!" Sandy shouted. "I'm going!" as she too took off on the next big wave, it just as perfect as that first one. Watching Sandy's athletic beauty move into a wave almost as pretty as her, was a joy every man should have once in his life. Two of nature's most graceful creations dancing with each other, moving in balance, almost singing to the other one.

I turned back at the top shoulder of her wave and tried to spot Tiwaka again. He wasn't on the wall anymore, but there seemed to be even more mynah birds, all watching the surf.

"Aloha dude!" The longboarder yelled over to me, paddling back out to catch another. I angled my path to meet up with him, glancing back to see Sandy exiting her wave, arms and fists high in the air proclaiming a surf victory.

This guy was older than me, perhaps quite a bit, but not elderly by any means. We met up and parked ourselves just beyond a big boil, where the onrushing wave energy below the surface pushed into a cave somewhere below and redirected up. They were always good as physical signposts in water that was moving with currents.

"Your friend just got a killer barrel!" he said. He turned to look back at her paddling out now.

I looked to see Sandy grinning and paddling hard to meet us in the lineup. "No one enjoys a big wave like my wife," for some reason I had to mention that she was my wife. Well, I knew why, this guy was kind of a looker himself. Always good to hit them up with the bad news early.

He sat up on his board and nodded. "Lucky man."

I smiled over to him and that's when I noticed his hair was still dry. How could that be? He had been surfing for over an hour before I even paddled out and he just had a big tube ride!

"Your hair," I said pointing. "Still dry?"

That got a big grin out of him. "Yep, it's a little contest I play with myself. See how many barrels I can get before my hair gets wet."

From my experience that had to be incredibly difficult, but then I wiped out more than most people. Sandy came up to us, sat up and shook her long hair, pulling it back quickly and retying her ponytail.

"Did you see my wave?" Her body looked incredible as she had her hands up in her hair.

"Awesome?" I asked, already knowing the answer.

"Double super-duper awesome," she confirmed, dropping her hands down to rest on her thighs. She was still catching her breath, but added "With sugar on top!"

Sandy looked over at the longboarder and took a moment before saying, "Uncle Vinny?"

He sat up a little straighter on his board at that. "One and only... Sandy?"

"Uncle Vinny!" Sandy practically screamed. "Where you been, Unc? We thought you had moved to the mainland or something."

"Wow, young lady, you sure grew up!" Uncle Vinny said, glancing back over to me with a knowing smile. "Last time I saw you was, like, I dunno, maybe grade school?"

"Gotta be!" Sandy looked over to me and introduced us. "Honey, Uncle Vinny Tortolano, famed helicopter pilot and longboard instructor."

I waved.

"Uncle Vinny, this is my wonderful husband ..." she paused and looked out to sea. "Set!"

Now, whenever you are having a nice relaxing conversation out in the ocean, bordering a reef on a big swell day and someone yells "Set!" it strikes a good dose of adrenaline into your bloodstream. That, and in my case, a hot spark of fear.

All three of us turned toward the outside waves and paddled as hard as we could. This was always a two-fold maneuver. First and foremost was avoiding getting caught inside where the waves would end up breaking – never any fun. Secondly, was why we were out here in the first place, to catch the 'wave of the day'.

I always liked to make sure the first problem was solved before considering the second benefit. Big waves had a way of holding you down underwater, pushing you into these infamous Waikiki coral caves or just beating on you for a minute or two. I had been rescued by another surfer in this very spot when I was a teenager and suddenly that memory found its way from the dark corners to the forefront of my mind.

I paddled as hard and swift as Sandy and Uncle Vinny and after a moment I lost my fear, seeing that we were going to end up in near perfect positioning to catch the first mondo wave. So, one fear down and the next popped into my mind.

"Sandy," I asked quickly. "Have you seen Tiwaka on the beach?"

"He's fine," she said, watching the wave approach. "Better than fine actually," she added, laying back down on her board and paddling out farther. Uncle Vinny sat there next to me and we looked at each other.

"Your wave dude," he offered, looking at the big wall growing taller. "This one might get my hair wet," he said and laughed uproariously.

"Cool!" I acknowledged and turned my board toward the beach, paddling hard to match the speed of the wave, watching it closely over my shoulder. I saw Sandy crest the big roller behind my wave and disappear on the other side, and Uncle Vinny rode the giant I was on up and over, watching me the entire time. He might have been yelling encouragement, but I couldn't hear him above the noise of the air rushing up the wall.

Catching a big wave must be a lot like taking a fast ball in the World Series. The batter puts himself in position, knowing what's coming and understands that the only way he is going to hit that ball is to focus on the pitcher. Good batters, I imagine, understand implicitly that the ball is itself a part of the pitcher as well. You watch his wind up, his eyes, the little nuances that might give you a hint as to where the ball is going and how fast. You gauge how his arm moves and then you watch as a small piece of him comes hurtling toward you, and your bat.

I was similarly focused on the wave, pitching to me on my board, as I rose up its crest backwards. It picked up the back of my board first as it lifted me up while accelerating me forward. How it did this, how it sucked out the water in front, how it made that boil roil with ferocity all told me where the ball was going. As I leapt to my feet, my toes clenching the wax on the board, finding the sweet spot of balance, I swung my bat, hoping to connect.

The exhilaration layer on top of a dose of fear tried to distract me, but as a good batter knows, you have to trust your instincts. Common sense assures that standing atop a ten foot, two hundred ton mountain of water chasing you across a shallower and shallower sharp reef is a bad idea. True, but that's only if you wipeout. I didn't intent to wipeout, I was going to hit that ball!

When I began surfing, I considered myself a success if I simply made the drop. The rest of the ride was bonus. Making the steep, vertical drop and getting to the bottom of the wave, still on my board, was the mark of a surfer. It was the most critical part perhaps. It was hitting that fast ball.

A brief instant of recognition flooded my mind as I began descending … this was the place that had hammered me years before, pushing me into one of those caves and darn near drowning me. In fact it was another big wave that had pushed me out of the cave, allowing me to flounder my way to the surface, there to get hammered by another four waves. Only two hundred yards from hundreds of thousands of people and it was the bravery of one local surfer, pulling me up and out of the water by my long hair that let me tell any stories at all. I wish I knew who he was. This time I would show him I could do it. I would show my fear that it wouldn't control me, despite how obnoxiously it might try.

In the World Series there is a competition of course, between pitcher and batter. I wouldn't extend the analogy that far when describing surfing, but I would say this. Any really great pitcher cannot help but be impressed when anyone hits a homerun off of him. He knows how good he is and how difficult it must be to connect, much less launch that ball into the upper stands. As I made the drop and crouched into my turn, setting up for the long wall ahead I smiled at the pitcher. I had taken a part of him, that ball, and put it high where he rarely got to go. Great heights are only realized when someone climbs them. So a surfer, in this way, enhances the beauty of a wave like this one.

I rose up from the flat areas in front of the wave and let my board climb half way back up the wall I was now traversing perpendicularly. The tall wave was aching to fold over on itself and the reef just to my right was going to make it all possible. My line seemed right on and I stood up straight, throwing my chest out a little and watching the big show.

Far up ahead I saw a guy in the water with a video camera. Cool! He looked to be positioned to catch my tube ride. Glancing up at the top of the feathering wall ahead I saw it was about to begin. I was glad that I would be able to share with someone what I was about to experience.

The front of my longboard at this point was well above the water's edge, hanging out in space four feet in front of me. I thought about hanging ten, but a wipeout here would mean certain bloodletting. I began to lean into a crouch as the wall finally threw itself forward, covering me in shadow as the barrel began.

It was just at that moment as the skyline of Waikiki soon became hidden behind a sheet of falling ocean, that a fast moving Tiwaka moved under the lip, banked and braked ahead of me, almost hitting the up rushing wall of water. He extended his talons just as I slid underneath him, grasping the nose of the board.

The wave immediately enveloped the both of us, me crouching and focused on surfing and Tiwaka leaning forward like a hood ornament, wings folded back now to better slip through the air.

The roaring of the water all around us was nothing compared to the music I was hearing now. I believe it was that from my dream, Pictures of Matchstick Men again. Here it was! Tiwaka and I riding a wave together! The video guy was quickly approaching off the right hand rail of my board, inches away actually. He was so good he could get this close.

Tiwaka took the opportunity, being the one with the middle name of Photogenic, to fold his talons into a shaka sign as he slid past the big lens. I did the same with my right hand and took the big risk of smiling directly into the camera. I did have a great grin, if I say so myself.

If my focus left the wave in front for even an instant it could be bad. And it almost was. My glance away let me drift up the face a bit too high, to where in just another instant we would get sucked up and over the falls, to certain near-destruction.

Tiwaka though, ever magical in his timing, extended his right wing to stall our upward movement and bring us back into line with the opening up ahead. Cowabunga! As they used to say before I was even born. I preferred Yabba Dabba Do actually. But I had to admit it was "Hallelujah" that moved past my lips right then.

~~~

Tiwaka, Sandy, Uncle Vinny and I eventually went in for some breakfast. We were all as high as you can get and not piss off the DEA. Best yet, it was a healthy high, renewable, green and kept the greenhouse gases minimized. Of course, at that point in my thoughts Tiwaka let out a big ol' Maui style burp. Except for that, we weren't polluting the atmosphere or our bodies!

Sandy and I were eating cake, just for fun. Tiwaka wanted some and I had to ask him, despite knowing the answer, "Do you really want chocolate cake, when you have a bowl full of lettuce?"

"Are you kidding?" Uncle Vinny asked.

It did seem an absurd choice.

The rest of the afternoon was spent riding the long rollers in front of the Royal Hawaiian Hotel. Tiwaka rode the front of my longboard, impressing everyone in the water and on the beach and even a few on their balconies. Mynah birds all through Kapiolani Park were swooning.

Diamond Head to our right framed the rest of the day of surfing, until another beautiful Waikiki sunset drove us back to the beach. We said aloha to all of our friends made that very day, picked up a very tired Tiwaka and put him on my shoulder.

Auntie Lois met us with Baby Kiawe at the Duke statue. It was her turn to surf now; her boogie board tucked under one arm and the diaper bag the other.

"That baby is too much fun!" Auntie Lois bragged. "Just like me!"

"You want to join us for dinner?" I asked.

"Cannot," Auntie Lois said, turning to look at the perfect surf. "Got some waves to catch before dark." She handed off the goodies and practically ran for the water.

I hung Baby Kiawe on my chest in the carrier, her giggling and squirming vibrating happily through my skin. Tiwaka watched me with interest.

"So Tiwaka," I began, looking at Sandy with a big smile. "What about all those macaws headed to Lahaina?"

Sandy grabbed me around my waist, hugging me as we all walked together. "Yes, Tiwaka. What will all those birds do on Maui?"

I looked up to see if I could spot his reaction, but I couldn't quite see his eyes up on my shoulders like he was. Passing a big overdone shop window I watched his reflection. He was slowly extending his wings, a sure sign of deep thought.

"Well," Tiwaka began. "I intend to teach those birds how to regain their confidence."

Sandy took a deep breath in surprise. We both couldn't get used to how well he was speaking. I shook my head as well, amazed. Again.

"After that we begin flight school. We'll bunk in the big banyan tree in Lahaina, at the harbor. After they graduate I thought we could start a fish spotting business."

Sandy and I had to consciously close our gaping mouths. Wow!

"You know, where we fly around and let the fishermen know where the schools are." He let out a celebratory squawk. "Can you imagine that, flying all the time?"

I had to admit that sounded pretty cool. Sandy put her head on my shoulder and we walked down another beautiful Waikiki sidewalk. The last of the sunset watched the three of us from the purple sky.

Tiwaka, still couldn't believe his good idea about fish spotting and added, "Imagine, getting paid to do what you love!"

Sandy walked another few steps before whispering to herself, to Tiwaka, Baby Kiawe and me and probably to the universe at large, "Love, Love, Love."

get the entire series!

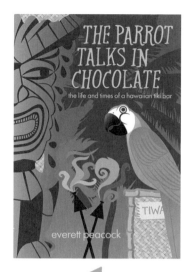

1

IN THE MIDDLE OF THE THIRD PLANET'S MOST WONDERFUL OF OCEANS

everett peacock

2

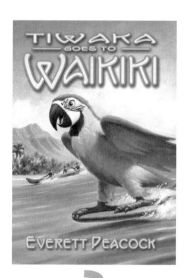

3

4

~~

ALOHA KAKOU

~~

Made in the USA
Thornton, CO
08/19/23 21:34:26